For all the boys

STEP INTO THE DARK

BRIDGET CROWLEY

Hodder
Children's
Books

a division of Hodder Headline Limited

A Catalogue record for this book is available from
the British Library

ISBN 0 340 84416 7

Typeset in Palatino by Avon Dataset Ltd,
Bidford-on-Avon, Warwickshire

Printed and bound in Great Britain by
Bookmarque Ltd, Croydon, Surrey

The paper and board used in this paperback by
Hodder Children's Books are natural recyclable products
made from wood grown in sustainable forests.
The manufacturing processes conform to the environmental
regulations of the country of origin.

Hodder Children's Books
A division of Hodder Headline Limited
338 Euston Road
London NW1 3BH

Chapter 1

'Haunted?' said Beetle.

He was sitting in The Hall with his feet up on the brown painted bench in front, ramming the last of the chewing gum into his mouth, watching a rehearsal of the Great Community Show.

'That's what they said,' said Greg. He rolled up a gum wrapper, aimed at one of the dim wall-lights – and missed.

'Don't believe it,' said Beetle, lowering his voice a little as the pianist glared at them over his glasses from his pool of light near the stage. 'There's no such thing – anyway, *who* said?'

'I dunno, man,' said Greg. 'I just heard it – you know.'

'Haunted! That's crap,' said Beetle.

'You shouldn't say words like that,' said a little girl in pink sparkly tights and frilly socks as she passed them. She was in a line of children from the tap-dancing class that emerged from backstage to wait for their mothers in the auditorium. She loitered by the two boys.

Beetle sighed.

'Go away, Kiley,' he said.

'My mum says you're awful, always using words like – like – *you* know – what you said. Anyway, it's all rubbish. I know, 'cos my gran said so.'

'What is?'

'The Hall being haunted, of cour—'

'Sssh,' said the pianist with another fierce glare.

Kiley's voice descended to a piercing whisper.

'Haunted – stupid. She says it's all stories.'

Kiley's gran worked in the market outside The Hall. She sold plates and cups and ornaments with lots of flowers and gold edges. She had worked there ever since she was a little girl in the war and knew everyone and everything there was to know. She even remembered when The Hall had been a proper music hall, with turns, professional turns, not like the awful stuff they put on nowadays, she said – except for Kiley's dancing class, of course.

'What're these stories supposed to be about, then, Miss Know-all?' said Beetle.

'Wouldn't you like to know,' said Kiley, who didn't know herself. 'If you want to know, ask my gran.

Anyway they're all rubbish, I told you. And I'm not Miss Know-all, so there.'

For once, Beetle couldn't face one of Kiley's 'oh yes you are, oh no I'm not' kinds of argument. He shrugged and looked away. Ben, the stage manager, peered round the curtain and beckoned to Greg. Greg jumped up and took his place on a little platform in front of the stage opposite the piano. On it stood a table and a gold-painted chair like a throne. It too was lit with a pool of light that made the tramlines through Greg's tight black curls glisten like tiny golden snakes curled round his head. Greg was master of ceremonies for the show. He introduced each act with a big flourish, a whack of his hammer on the table, and lots of long words that Beetle didn't understand and wasn't sure Greg did either.

There were more tap dancers who really could dance a bit, not like Kiley who wobbled all over when she tried to do 'wings'. There was Jamey Rogers from the next street who juggled up a storm with six oranges from the market, the Wilson Brothers who did a funny turn and who hadn't made anyone laugh in a hundred years but were still trying, a steel band, and Tamar, who sang.

Tamar was sixteen, tall, with long straight hair that shimmered the colour of moonlight on the lake in the park at night, and eyes like the black cat next door, ebony flecked with gold. She sang strange chanting songs that swung from high, thin sounds like the wind down by the river, to deep echoing sighs that whispered round the shadows of The Hall and made Beetle's spine tingle. When she sang, she wore a velvet waistcoat with tiny mirrors in it that winked in the coloured lights, a long swishy skirt like a rainbow and little gold shoes on little golden-brown feet. Beetle always listened to her spellbound, hardly moving.

Kiley went to sit with her mother and two tiny little girls all in shiny white, who were also from the dancing class. Beetle waited for Greg to make his stupendous, splendiferous, sensational announcement for the Senior Citizens Choir – First World War Favourites, loud if a bit out of tune. Then they settled in the back row to practise hitting the wall-lights again with silver chewing-gum paper.

'Oi!' said a voice in a hoarse whisper. 'Pack it in! Unless you want to clean up.'

Old Mitch, the caretaker, was very fussy about his hall. The dark brown floor always gleamed with wax, even if the paint was shabby and the tiles out in the hallway were cracked. Beetle slipped across, picked up the paper and stuffed it into his pocket.

Suddenly, another paper pellet hit him on the shoulder. He looked up. Zak, the Hall technician, was grinning down at him from the top balcony, high, high above.

No one else was allowed up there, certainly not 'unaccompanied kids'. The floor was dangerous, loose boards on top of old plaster. Lethal. So said Old Mitch. Only the staff of The Hall were allowed to go up to the top balcony, but that didn't stop Beetle sneaking up there with Zak whenever he got the chance.

At the back of the balcony, raked up high on a rickety platform facing down towards the stage of The Hall, was the lighting desk. Sometimes, Zak would let Beetle work the dimmer, quietly sliding the knobs that dimmed or brightened the lights, turned the colour wheels, hit one person on the stage with a blinding spotlight, or plunged all the performers below into a kind of black pit – total blackout. That was fun. They all squawked and bashed about in the dark like a lot of old hens, while Zak and Beetle tried not to laugh as they called out, 'Sorry! Be right with you . . . Tech problems . . .' Then the cast on stage would witter on about being irresponsible . . . not fit to do the job . . . the kind of thing grown-ups always said, as if they never made mistakes.

From below, Beetle could just make out the skull and crossbones on Zak's tight-fitting T-shirt. His six earrings flashed in the lights from the stage as he jerked his head upwards.

'You coming up?'

He mouthed the words silently. Beetle gave him two thumbs up.

'Won't catch me going up there,' said Greg.

'Frightened the ghosties'll get you?' said Beetle.

Greg gave him a mock punch.

'Just couldn't face all those stairs,' he said.

'Oh yeah?'

'Yeah!'

Zak gave a quiet whistle from above and mouthed:

'Today would be nice. I've got to aim some lamps before I go.'

Beetle gave him another two thumbs and slid out through the double doors at the back of The Hall.

The stone stairs that wound up through the old Hall to the top balcony were dark and draughty. A sickly smell of escaping gas from the poky little kitchen at one side of the hallway seemed to ooze upwards and mix with other smells of damp and disinfectant. Cobwebs hung in lank festoons from the ceiling far above and a huge patch of peeling paint dangled from the wall and brushed his face as he passed, taking the stairs two at a time. Even the padding sound of his trainers seemed to echo up and down the cavernous stairwell. He wasn't scared but somehow he didn't want to hang around. There was one particular bend in the stairs he always hurried round specially fast, where an old door loomed out of the shadows. It seemed to tip forward off the wall, as if it might creak open on its own at any moment. If there really were ghosts in The Hall, that's where . . . Beetle gave the door a kick as he passed, just to show he didn't believe a word of the story. Then he belted like lightning up to the top and in through the double doors on to the balcony with a crash.

'Sssh,' said Zak. 'Choir's still giving us *Daisy, Daisy* – well, it makes a change.'

He rolled his eyes upwards in disbelief.

'Seriously,' he said, 'we can carry on while they're singing if we're quiet. I'll call you the numbers.'

Zak knew the lighting rig and the board inside out and backwards. He would change the positions of the lamps balanced on the narrow balcony rail, leaning out over the void without turning a hair of his long straight pony-tail, while Beetle sat at the board, trying to keep his stomach from churning in case Zak should fall.

Beetle knew the numbers by heart, which knob on the board matched which lamp hanging over the audience, but it was good having Zak quietly calling them to him one at a time, so they could test that each lamp was working. It gave Beetle a special feeling of belonging up here, busy, involved, and strangely apart from what was going on down below. It was as if what was happening on the stage was in a different world that only existed because he and Zak lit it up from here. It was as if, with one swift slide of the dimmer, the stage and all the glitter below would vanish, leaving him and Zak in the proper world up here.

'I said "five",' said Zak in a fierce whisper. 'Think what you're doing.'

'Five's up,' said Beetle, pushing the knob up and down and staring across at the lamp. Nothing happened.

'Bulb's gone,' said Zak, with a word Kiley's mum would not approve of. He came back along the balcony and poked around among the empty boxes and other rubbish behind the lighting board.

'Nope, none here,' he said. 'I'll have to go down and get one from the store. Shan't be a tick.'

He pushed out through the doors and Beetle heard him bounding down the stairs three or four at a time on his long, skinny legs.

The choir was just finishing. Beetle looked down at the stage from behind the lighting desk. The conductor was giving them a few last-minute instructions. Old Mitch was tidying up with Brian from the day centre up the road, but who seemed to spend all his time in The Hall. Brian liked Mitch and doing odd jobs. Sometimes he made tea that he spilt all over the place but that everyone was glad of. Beetle could hear the two of them chuntering on together about messy people and nuisances and stuff. Gradually the auditorium emptied. Kiley's mum followed Greg backstage with the three little girls. Only Tamar stood alone in the spotlight by the piano. She never joined in the gossip and bustle backstage, but waited quietly for her mother to go home with her.

Beetle began to fiddle about with the dimmers to keep himself company, but Zak had turned most of them off before he went downstairs. It was cold on the balcony, in spite of the evening sun outside in the market, and Zak seemed to be taking his time. It was dark too. Black paint covered the windows, but a few scratches let in small beams of light here and there, picking out the grey plaster dust that covered the rickety old benches. A dim exit light cast a long shadow on the damp-spotted wall – a long, box-shaped shadow . . . Somewhere, something seemed to be dripping, plop . . . plop.

Beetle shook himself, squeezed out from behind the dimmer and went down the two or three steps to look over the edge of the balcony. Tamar was still sitting calmly on the piano stool. Perhaps he would call out to her, just for company. But suddenly, the thought of his voice echoing out over the huge space between them was too much – and he might startle her. The balcony ran round three sides of The Hall and had an iron railing to stop you falling over – but the fancy pattern was full of gaps. If you really wanted to fall over, you only had to bend down and put your head through and then your shoulders and . . . When you looked down, it took your breath away, it was so far to fall – past the great gas chandeliers, past the lower balcony, past the shaded lights on the walls beneath, past the tall gilt mirrors that were not glass at all, but only made of shiny tin – down, down, on to the benches on the floor far below.

How much longer was Zak going to be? Beetle straightened up and turned to go back to the board.

A flash of white caught his eye from the end of the balcony towards the stage. Beetle stopped, horrified. A little girl stood there. It was one of the little girls in white that Beetle had seen with Kiley's mum, he was sure. She must have passed him while he was looking down at Tamar. What should he do? It was dangerous down that end of the balcony, he knew. The floor was rotten.

'Hey,' said Beetle, calling softly. He didn't want to frighten the child. She was reaching up to lean over the balcony rail, but it was almost as tall as she was. 'Hey, you shouldn't be up here. Come over this way. Come to me, I'll take you downstairs.'

Beetle started to move towards the child, slowly and carefully, picking his way from board to board, when he heard Zak pounding up the stairs and in through the doors.

'Watch it,' he said, turning quickly. 'There's one of the dancing class kids leaning over the balcony down at the end there. Don't frighten her or she might fall.'

'Where?' said Zak.

'Down there.'

Beetle turned back and pointed. The balcony was empty. He caught his breath. She hadn't put her head through the railing and fallen, had she? But he would have heard the crash. He peered over to make sure.

'Which one was it?'

'Dunno. Hard to tell in the dark, but I think she was with Kiley, earlier.'

'I'll have a word with the dancing teacher tomorrow,' said Zak. 'They shouldn't be up here.'

'But where did she go?' said Beetle. 'She didn't go through the doors, did she?'

Zak shrugged and started to replace the bulb in the dead lamp.

'No,' he said. 'I'd have passed her on the stairs if she had. She must've gone down the back way. There's another door behind the curtains at the end there.'

Beetle started towards the end of the balcony.

'Don't even think about it,' said Zak. 'You'll go through the floor. Just take my word for it, there's a door behind those curtains and stairs that lead down to the dressing-rooms, backstage. The door should be locked. I'll ask Old Mitch about it. If one of those kids has found it, you can bet the others'll be up here tomorrow, and we can't have kids up here, it's not safe.'

Beetle pulled himself up to his full height in case Zak suddenly remembered how old he was, but all Zak said was:

'Let's get on with it. I want to go down to the pub

tonight, not next week. I've got a gig.'

Zak played lead guitar in a rock group. Ellsteef, they were called. They were wicked. When his mum said she was working late, Beetle would listen outside the pub, sitting on the pavement.

'Come on,' said Zak again, as he clipped the lamp shut.

Beetle tested it. A brilliant gold light shot up to the ceiling. Zak swivelled it back into place, tightened it up, focused it, ran nimbly back along the benches avoiding the floor, and switched off the board.

'Let's go, sunshine,' he said. 'That'll do for tonight. I'll talk to Old Mitch in the morning about that door.'

Zak swung his bomber jacket over his shoulder. They raced down the stairs and pushed out into the street. The market was closed and evening was drawing in. There was no sign of any of the dancing-class kids with their mothers. Even the senior citizens were home eating their tea.

Beetle left Zak at the pub door and went home via the burger bar. Lighting was hungry work.

Chapter 2

Greg and Beetle were out in the market, sharing a bag of chips well laced with vinegar and tomato sauce. They tangled fingers over the last chip, rolled the bag up into a ball and Beetle drop-kicked it into a nearby skip.

'Oi, knock it off,' said the man selling tools and batteries and lengths of plastic chain. 'You'll have this lot over if you don't watch it.'

'Sorry guv,' said Beetle, and they ambled along the pavement behind market barrows piled with shiny fruit or toys or radios or washing-up liquid and tins of biscuits or colourful clothes fluttering high up in the sun. They dodged and scuffled and jostled each other off the pavement. When they came to some scaffolding shoring up an old building, all in one swift movement, Greg pulled himself up on a cross bar, somersaulted round it and dropped off. He landed awkwardly and almost knocked over a pile

14

of plates nicely balanced as part of a display on the china stall.

'Buzz off, you two,' said Kiley's gran. 'You're not safe, you're not. If you break anything, you'll have to pay for it.'

'Oooh, if you break anything you'll have to pay for it,' said Greg, wagging a finger, mimicking her in a high, silly voice. She flapped at him with a duster she kept handy for the china.

'Don't you be so cheeky,' she said. 'I'll have a word with your dad when I see him next.'

'Yeah?'

'The word's yes,' she said, 'and yes, I will. Trouble with you is you haven't got enough to do. When I was your age . . .'

'We know,' said Greg with a grin, dancing about doing suitable actions, 'you did all the washing without a washing machine, cleaned the house on your hands and knees, cooked the dinner, did your homework like a good girl and ran the market single-handed. And we don't know we're alive, nowadays.'

He clapped his hand to his chest and flung his head back in a melodramatic pose.

Kiley's gran laughed.

'Oh, go on with you,' she said.

'That's the trouble,' said Greg. 'Where do we go

to? There's nothing to do round here, and it's hours till tonight's rehearsal.'

Kiley's gran gave him an old-fashioned look.

'Bored, are you?' she said. 'I don't know. Kids today. Trouble is . . . Tell you what, could you mind the stall for me a minute, Beetle? I need to pop up to the supermarket for some stuff for tea, and Mr Ginley's gone early.'

Mr Ginley ran the fruit and veg stall next to Kiley's gran's and sometimes looked after it for her.

'Us?' said Greg. 'Can't Kiley do it?'

'Kiley's at home where she should be, not wandering the streets like some people,' said her gran. 'Anyway, she's much too little. Come on, are you going to give me a hand or what?'

' 'Course we are,' said Beetle. 'Come on, Greg, you told me Jamey Rogers had been giving you lessons. Show me how you juggle plates.'

Kiley's gran's face was a study.

'You dare,' she said.

'Only joking,' said Beetle.

'Hmm. I know you and your jokes. Just you remember . . .' she said, jabbing her finger at a notice at the front of the stall.

'We know,' said Greg, imitating her again, ' "all breakages have to be paid for." '

With another flap, this time of the apron she took off and stowed in a box full of paper shavings under the stall, she hurried off up the street, smiling and calling out to everyone in the market on the way. She disappeared into the supermarket with a shriek and a cackle at some saucy remark from the CD and cassettes man.

Beetle looked at the stall, straightened up a pile of china and rearranged some ornaments. He poked about in a bin full of china mugs. He put some of the brighter ones on top so they really showed up. Then he tried making all the handles face one way.

'What you bothering with all that for?' said Greg from the scaffolding where he was balancing spreadeagled on his stomach. 'It looks OK as it is.'

'Got to get things looking right,' said Beetle.

'What difference does it make?' said Greg.

'It just – it just looks better,' said Beetle.

A young woman in brown stretch pants and with blonde hair and 'roots' stopped at the stall.

'These are nice,' she said. 'Cheap too. I like the colours. They'll do for my sister's birthday.'

She picked out six of the brightest mugs from the top of the bin and handed them to Beetle to wrap carefully in newspaper. He gave Greg an 'I told you so' look.

'Lovely,' said the girl. 'How much?'

Greg swung down from the scaffolding.

'One-twenty-five each. How many have you got?'

'Six,' said the girl.

Greg scratched his head.

'Six times £1.25 . . .' he said, 'let's see . . .'

'Seven pounds fifty. Don't you know anything?' said a high-pitched voice that sounded as if it always wore frilly socks. It was Kiley.

'Fancy not knowing that.'

''Course we knew,' said Greg.

'Oh yes,' said Kiley. '*I* think. You can't neither of you do sums, you're just stupid.'

'Oh no we're—' said Beetle and Greg together.

'Excuse me. If I could just have my mugs please,' said the blonde girl. 'Could you have your argument later?'

'Sorry,' said Beetle.

The girl paid him and hurried off.

'You nearly lost us that deal,' said Greg, 'butting in like that.'

The 'oh no I didn't-ing' was about to start again when Kiley's gran returned. She plonked a kiss on Kiley's head. Beetle and Greg exchanged a look.

'Where's your mum?' said Kiley's gran.

'Gone into Woolies. She won't be long. I've come to see you.'

She took her gran's hand and swung it backwards and forwards.

'Beetle just sold six mugs to some girl,' said Greg.

'Quite a salesman. I'll have to leave you in charge more often, young Beetle,' said Kiley's gran.

'Not if *she's* here,' said Greg.

He jerked his head at Kiley.

'What do you mean, Greg Thomas?' said Kiley's gran. 'What's she done to you?'

'Nothing,' said Kiley. 'He's just narked because I can do sums and they can't. Look at my new socks, Gran. Aren't they beautiful?'

'They're gross, man,' said Greg. 'They look like those frill things round the chops in the butchers.'

Kiley's face crinkled up ready to cry.

'Don't take any notice of him, love,' said her gran. 'They're beautiful. I never had socks like that when I was a girl, I can tell you.'

'What were they like, then?' said Beetle. He liked stories of long ago, of the war-time when the bombs were falling and people had to sleep in air-raid shelters or down in the tube stations and there weren't any bananas.

'Grey,' said Kiley's gran. 'Grey mostly. Well, mine

were. I wore my brother's cast-offs if there was anything left of them by the time he'd finished. My mum, that's your great-gran, Kiley, she used to mend them. Took her hours. All lumpy they were. Big lumps of darning on your heels so your shoes felt tight. And they, kind of – bulged over the back. Oh dear – those were the days.'

Beetle wasn't sure how grey lumpy socks could mean better days, though his own were far from white and had holes in the heels.

'I reckon it's better now,' he said, 'with socks of your own, and sports socks and all that.'

'Don't you believe it,' said Kiley's gran. 'We've got so much we don't know what to do with it all. And we're no happier, I can tell you.'

'I am,' said Kiley. 'I like these better than grey ones that bulge.'

' 'Course you do,' said her gran, 'they're lovely. But just the same . . .'

'You remember The Hall in those days, don't you?' said Beetle.

'I do,' she said.

'What was it like then?'

'Well in some ways it wasn't as – well, smart.'

'Not as smart? But the paint's peeling off everywhere now except in the auditorium and the balcony's not safe and . . .'

'Yes, but at least it's *been* painted, and there's those lovely big gas chandeliers that the Museum lent them when they did the renovations, and nice blue velvet curtains on the stage. There was tatty old things in those days. But the acts – oh, the acts were marvellous.'

'Good as us?' said Greg, with a grin.

Kiley's gran sniffed. Kiley looked up from admiring her socks and took her hand.

'And there isn't a ghost, is there, Gran?'

' 'Course not, love. Whatever gave you that idea?'

'*They* said.'

'What? Have you been trying to frighten Kiley?' She sounded really angry.

'No,' said Beetle.

'Kiley, you're a little liar,' said Greg.

'No, I'm not. You are. You were saying about it, yesterday, at The Hall.'

'And you said your gran said—'

'Ask your gran, you said,' said Beetle and Greg at the same time.

'Shut up, all of you,' said Kiley's gran. 'Listen to me, you two. I won't have Kiley being frightened.'

'We didn't,' said Beetle. 'She heard us talking and . . .'

'Shoved her nose in, as usual,' said Greg.

'You be quiet, Greg,' said her gran as Kiley went red and looked as if she might explode.

'Why did you tell them to ask me, Kiley?'

'Because you were telling Mum, last Christmas. You did. You did. I heard you.'

'All right, all right. So I did. *And* I told her it was rubbish, didn't I?'

'Yes,' said Kiley, then smugly to the boys, 'told you so.'

'It was just silly Christmas stories. If there was really a ghost I wouldn't have talked about it with you there, not with you going to The Hall for your dancing class so often. I don't want you scared.'

'I wouldn't be scared. I'm not scared of anything.'

'Huh. Anyway, take a pretty brave ghost to take on all you lot in that dancing class,' said Greg. 'Waaah!'

He made a horrible face and waved his hands in Kiley's face. She stuck out her tongue and her gran tutted and pulled her back by the shoulder.

Beetle laughed.

'And I told you, didn't I, young Kiley?' he said. 'No such thing.'

Just then, Zak came hurrying up the market, his

guitar case slung on his back. He looked worried and he hadn't shaved, but when he saw Beetle, his thin face broke into a big grin.

'Hey, Beetle, am I glad to see you. Listen, I've got an extra rehearsal with the band tonight. It's for something really big. It's not for long, but I can't miss it.'

'But we've got a rehearsal for the show, too.'

'I know. Look, could you – do you think . . .'

Beetle's eyes grew wide.

'Do it on my own?'

Zak nodded. Beetle flushed with pleasure to think Zak thought him capable of managing the whole rehearsal single-handed.

'It's all set up. The lighting plot is on the desk, and it's dead simple for most things. You know how to set up a cue during the state before, don't you?'

Beetle thought for a moment.

'Put up one set of lights on one dimmer, and set up the next lot on the second dimmer, switch over on the cue and set up again on the one you've just taken down.'

'That's right. You've done it with me there and the cues aren't very fast, not for this show. And just hold your blackouts till Ben gives you the cue over the headphones.'

'OK. What about cross-fades?'

'You can do cross-fades, no sweat. Just keep steady, one hand up, the other down and don't let them dip as they pass. Come on, Beetle. You've done them before.'

Beetle swallowed. He had done them before, but not with everyone there.

'OK.'

'Great. I'll come down with you and switch on. I don't want you touching the mains. I'll help you set up the first two cues and then leave you to it. If I'm not back when they've finished, just bring down the dimmers and leave them. I'll come back and switch off later.'

'Oh – cool. Coming, Greg?'

'No, thanks. I'm an actor, me. You can keep all that electrics stuff. Anyway I've got to go home first, to pick up my costume.'

'OK. See you later.'

Beetle and Zak went off together towards The Hall at a brisk jog.

'He's clever at all that lighting, that Beetle, isn't he?' said Kiley's gran.

'And at selling china,' said Greg. 'He just shifted those mugs so's you could see them better and bob's your uncle.'

'Well, he can't add up for toffee,' said Kiley. 'And *I* think he's stupid.'

'At least he doesn't wear chop frills round his ankles,' said Greg in a disgusted tone, and beat it before Kiley could get a word in.

Chapter 3

Zak and Beetle turned the corner. Outside The Hall stood Tamar. She was pressed into a corner of the wall, looking down, trying to cover her face with her veil. Two big lads stood in front of her, leaning towards her, one with his hand on the wall blocking her escape. They wore high-tops, combats and shiny padded jackets, khaki with orange linings, and their heads were shaved. They were laughing, trying to twitch the veil away from Tamar's fingers as she jerked her head from side to side to evade them.

'Come on, give us a look!'

'No harm in looking, is there?'

'What do you want to hide yourself away for – nice little bit of Turkish delight like you?'

Beetle heard a hiss as Zak drew a breath. Then Zak hurled himself forward and shoved himself between them and Tamar.

'Get lost,' he said, looking the biggest one squarely

in the eye. Beetle had never seen him look angry before, but now his whole skinny body was taut with rage. 'Leave her alone.'

'Suppose *you* get lost,' said the boy slowly, turning to face him with a nasty look in his eye.

'I said, leave her alone,' said Zak. Still looking straight at the boy, he put a hand on Tamar's shoulder and pushed her gently forward towards Beetle. Quickly, Beetle hurried her through the door of The Hall, then turned back to see if Zak was all right.

'I wouldn't if I were you,' he heard Zak say.

'Gonna hit us with your guitar-box then, are you, big man – or give us a tune?'

'It wouldn't be the guitar I hit you with,' said Zak.

Zak might be thin, but he was strong, much taller and older than the two lads. Beetle could see they didn't relish the idea of a punch.

'Quite a hero, aren't we?' said one, with a sneer.

'No,' said Zak. 'I just do what I have to. Now, are you gonna leave it?'

The lads shrugged and turned away. They slouched off, muttering to each other, giving Zak and Beetle two fingers over their shoulders as they went.

Zak watched them go. Beetle looked up at him.

'That sorted them,' he said.

'I hate having to do all that stuff,' said Zak, and angrily pushed into The Hall.

He looked at Tamar, who still kept her eyes on the ground and tugged at her veil.

'I am not Turkish, I am a Kurd,' she said.

'I know. You all right?' he said.

'Yes, yes,' she said, but Beetle could see she was shaking a little. 'Thank you for helping me. They would not really hurt me I think, but . . .'

'I wouldn't bank on that,' said Zak. Then, 'No, no,' he said quickly, as she glanced up at him with anxious eyes, 'I guess you're right. They were all mouth. Don't worry about it.'

But Beetle could see he was only saying it to reassure her. She nodded, trying to smile.

'Where's your mum?' said Beetle. 'You usually come with her, don't you?'

Tamar gave a little laugh.

'Serves me right, I suppose,' she said. 'I told her I was quite old enough to come on my own. We had a bit of – well, an argument, but she gave in. She says going to school is one thing, but here in the evening when it is getting dark . . . I should have listened.'

'You shouldn't have to worry about all – all that,' said Zak, frowning. 'If I can walk up the street with no bother, you should be able to too. I've seen those

28

two before. What they don't understand, they can't leave alone.'

'Yeah,' said Beetle. 'Greg's brother had trouble with them too. They're in his class at school – 'cept they never seem to go.'

Tamar looked sad.

'I am not so difficult to understand,' she said.

' 'Course not,' said Zak. 'And you can sing up a storm.'

Tamar smiled.

'Thank you,' she said.

'What about getting home?' said Zak.

'My mother is coming,' she said, with a little sigh. 'I confess, I am quite glad now. But I'm quite sure it would be all right, anyway.'

'It had better be,' said Zak. 'They'd better not try anything . . .'

'They were only teasing, really, I – I'm sure,' said Tamar. 'But thank you, my mother will be here. And oh, I think – I think I will not tell her about – about the boys . . .'

Zak and Beetle nodded their understanding and she went down the dingy passage to the room behind the kitchen and at the side of the auditorium where the cast of the show were gathering. Zak looked after her.

'You like her, don't you,' said Beetle.

'She's all right,' said Zak with a shrug, but going a bit pink. 'I like her singing. Come on, or I'll be late.'

They raced up the stairs and Zak switched on. Down in the auditorium the pianist was tinkling away, warming up. Ben Starkey was running a finger down his clip-board. Ben was stage manager, but worked full time at The Hall too, teaching and organizing all the activities that went on in the community centre, classes in everything from art to adult literacy, and clubs and groups. Happily for Beetle, what Ben liked doing best was putting on shows by people in the neighbourhood themselves, or getting in professional companies to perform, so there was always something going on that needed lighting.

'You OK if I leave you now?' said Zak.

'Yep,' said Beetle.

'I'll be back as soon as I can, but if they finish before I get here, just bring down the dimmers. Don't touch the mains, OK?'

'OK.'

He picked up his guitar and was gone.

Sitting alone on the shadowy balcony, Beetle suddenly needed to keep his courage up. What if he made a mess of it? No, of course he wouldn't, cross-fades were no sweat – he'd better believe it. He put on the headphones that put him in touch with Ben, who always stood in the corner of the stage while the show was running. He spoke into the little mike that stuck up just in front of his nose.

'Hullo and good evening,' he said in a joking voice, as much like Zak as he could manage. 'Anyone home?'

'Yes, hi!'

Ben looked up in surprise. He was standing in the middle of the empty stage in the flat square of light cast by the working lights.

'Oh it's you, young Beetle,' he said through the headphones. 'I'd forgotten. Zak told me you'd be doing this rehearsal. You OK?'

'Sure,' said Beetle, trying not to sound too excited.

'We're ready down here,' said Ben, 'except for half the dancing class, the master of ceremonies and a couple of comedians. Then we can start. Nothing changes.'

Stage crews, in Ben's book, were always ready long before the cast. The theatre would be fine if it weren't for the actors, he said.

Just then the auditorium doors banged and Greg swept into The Hall resplendent in his Victorian costume. He took his place in the huge chair in front of the stage. The tight-fitting Victorian-style trousers and high collar looked extremely uncomfortable to Beetle. He was glad to be up where he was, wearing what he was wearing and doing what he was doing. No way could he put on that fancy gear and sit in the spotlight. Funny how Greg seemed to love it. He was welcome to it. Sitting up here with his fingers on a dimmer board was the place to be.

'Everyone's ready when you are,' said Greg to Ben, nodding towards the back of the stage.

'OK, let's go,' came the reply. Then, through the headphones, 'Stand by elex.'

'Standing by,' said Beetle, giving himself a little hug inside as he listened to Ben giving other instructions backstage. He could hear a lot of little voices in the background like chattering chickens and then Ben trying to shut them up. The dancing teacher, Miss James, looking elegant but just a little hassled, slipped through the pass door to watch her 'babes'. Ben switched off the working lights and gave the first cue.

'Go house. Stand by Q1.'

'House gone. Standing by Q1.'

Beetle pulled down the dimmer steadily and firmly and the auditorium dissolved into darkness.

'Tabs going up.'

The curtains at the front of the stage parted with as much of a swish as Ben could manage by just pulling on the ropes. There were no fancy power-driven aids for moving scenery here at The Hall – just brawn. Even Beetle's dimmer board was archaic.

'Go Q1.'

Beetle pushed up the first dimmer and his mouth went up with it in a huge grin. The children of the dancing class smiled up, it seemed, directly at him, their sequins and satins twinkling and gleaming in the soft, bright light that he, just he, had given them. Even Kiley looked – well, certainly not beautiful, but a lot better than usual. She still couldn't do wings though. Beetle giggled to himself as she wobbled about, then remembered his responsibilities and started to check up on the lighting cues.

The show was the usual chaos of a first dress rehearsal. Things that had always gone well before went wrong now. People missed their cues and blamed everyone else. Jamie had trouble with his brand new Indian clubs. The comedians actually got a laugh they hadn't intended when one of them tripped and fell smack on his bottom in the middle of their closing song. He stormed off and threatened never to appear again.

'Is that a promise?' Beetle heard Ben mutter over the headphones.

Beetle laughed but had his work cut out to keep up with the cues, cutting backwards and forwards through the show as things had to be repeated 'from the top'. A couple of cross-fades had been a bit wobbly, but maybe no one had noticed. At the end of their number, the dancing class children, restless and excited, filed into the auditorium to watch the rest of the rehearsal. They rattled sweet papers and crisp packets, whispering and giggling. Old Mitch and Brian would have something to moan about later.

Then it was Tamar's turn to sing.

Beetle was so busy setting up the board that Greg's voice yelling from below took him by surprise.

'Hey, man! Beetle! Give us a light. What you doing, leaving me in the dark?'

For a moment, Beetle panicked. Where had he gone wrong? What had he missed? The lighting plot slithered to the floor and he nearly choked on the lead from the headphones as he bent down to retrieve it.

Ben's voice came over the headphones.

'Come on, Beetle. What are you up to? I gave you Q10.'

'Q10 gone,' said Beetle, pushing wildly at the dimmer switch, hoping for the best.

Nothing happened.

Far below he heard Kiley's strident whisper, 'It's that stupid Beetle, making mistakes again. And he can't do sums, neither.'

Beetle bad-mouthed her silently and began to sweat.

He took a deep breath, checked the plot again quickly, flicked a few switches and lo and behold, when he looked over, Greg's moon-face was beaming up at him from a pool of pink light. Very flattering, thought Beetle, wiping damp hands on his baggy jeans. That had been a nasty moment. He'd get Kiley later.

'Sorry, Ben,' he whispered into his mike, 'I just got two cues—'

'No chatting over the 'phones during the show, remember?' said Ben firmly. 'This isn't BT.'

Then he relented.

'Don't worry, Beetle, you're doing fine. Just keep calm.'

'OK,' said Beetle, angry with himself for screwing up, but pleased he was 'doing fine'. Just as well it was only a rehearsal though.

Then he heard Greg from below:

'Sugar and spice and everything nice. A little lady from far away, but close to your hearts, ladies and gentlemen. Here she is, your own, your very own, delicious, delightful, delectable – Tamar!'

Beetle grinned. Blacked out or not, Greg was on top form. But he must concentrate. This one mustn't go wrong or Zak would never forgive him.

Tamar began to clap a rhythm very quietly, her little mirrors twinkling in the soft, gold light that Beetle sent down to her, making her teeth flash white and her eyes glow. She began to sway almost imperceptibly. Even the dancing class children stopped crunching and listened.

In the hush, Beetle felt the tingling at the back of his neck that he had felt before when he listened to Tamar sing – it was the strange, haunting way her voice swooped and spiralled from the high, reed-like notes down to deep, throbbing tones that echoed and shivered round the old Hall. Just as his lights could sweep into shadows, dispelling them or calling them up, Tamar's voice seemed to make light and shadows in the air. He was entranced. Ben's voice giving him a cue to change the colour of her spotlight to deep blue made him jump. He pulled himself together. Smoothly, without a single jerk or judder, he cross-faded in a way that even Zak would be proud of.

The Hall became dark and mysterious. As he glanced up, something caught his eye.

A moment ago he had been sweating, now, suddenly, he went cold. At the far end of the balcony stood that dancing class kid again. This time she was really leaning out into space through a gap in the railings, her arms outstretched towards the stage. She could easily slip through. Beetle was furious. Why hadn't Old Mitch locked the door?

'Ben! Hullo, Ben!' he said in an urgent whisper. 'I've got an emergency up here.'

But Ben didn't answer. Well, he must do something even if it meant missing more cues. Angrily, Beetle pulled off his headphones and started down the steps towards the edge of the balcony. He must get to the child before she slipped over or went through the floorboards. He knew that Zak always ran along the benches which had been placed where the floor was strongest. He jumped up on the first bench, starting to hurry down the side of the balcony towards the little girl, but it was dark. Just a faint blue light spilled up from the stage. He tried to run, but stumbled, and slowed down, feeling along the bench with his foot. He could hear Tamar's voice curling and swooping around and above him. The child gave a silent cry and leant further forward, clapping her hands out into the space. It was as if she had a small circle of light of her own, as her dress caught the blue iridescence from below. She opened her mouth, seeming to call out to someone below, someone on the stage perhaps, but no sound came.

In a fierce whisper, Beetle said, 'Sssh. Keep still. Keep still, I said. Just don't move.'

Quickly, the little girl drew back and turned her head. She stared at him in alarm, her great eyes wide with fear, her hands to her face. For a moment, she seemed to stare straight into his eyes, holding him still. Her mouth trembled as if she wanted to speak but couldn't. Beetle held his breath as she seemed to sway against the balcony rail – would it hold? Cautiously, he put out a hand towards her but she started away from him up the steps behind her.

'It's all right,' he said, desperately. 'I'm not going to hurt you – but it's not safe. Just keep still, I'm coming to help you.'

He took a leap forward to the next bench, but he misjudged the distance in the dark. His foot slipped and he fell. The floorboard gave way and his leg disappeared in a cloud of plaster dust from below. He grabbed the bench and held on, praying that he wouldn't go right through. Oddly, Tamar's voice went on as if nothing had happened, but over it he thought he heard the curtain at the end of the balcony rattle and the door slam.

He looked round. The child had gone.

He heaved himself up and sat on the bench for a moment. He could see a patch of blood seeping through his jeans and he had splinters in his hands, but carefully he began to feel his way back towards the switchboard. Tamar finished singing. He had missed another cue and there would be another straight afterwards. Now Ben would be furious. Again, he tried to hurry, but he was shaking and dropped the headphones. He could hear Ben's voice urgently giving cues but he couldn't be sure now where he was in the plot. At last he got the headphones on.

'Sorry, Ben – sorry. Where are—'

'For crying out loud, Beetle, what's the matter with you? You've missed three cues, for goodness' sake.'

'Sorry, I—'

'Just get it together, will you. You should be on Cue 17. Just put anything up for now, and catch up. It's the steel band next.'

That was easy enough – everything up, as much light as possible. Beetle pushed up every dimmer he could lay his splintery hands on and a great surge of light burst upwards. He sighed with relief and lay his head on the board for a minute, getting his breath. Then he looked along the balcony. The far end was dark and still.

The rest of the show was simple, but Beetle felt like – like crap. He was going to have to face Ben and tell him about the broken board. Ben might not be too angry when he knew about the little girl, but then he'd have to tell Zak he had missed Tamar's last two light changes and spoilt the mood of her act. He sat miserably, digging a splinter out of his thumb and sucking it, waiting for the steel band to finish . . . Well, at least it was only a dress rehearsal.

Chapter 4

Beetle pulled down the dimmers, tidied his cue sheets, hung his head-set over the arm of a nearby spotlight and went downstairs. He gave the leaning door a savage kick as he passed. Why had that stupid kid had to get herself up there again, making trouble?

The leaning door creaked a little as he passed but Beetle ignored it, and stumped on down the echoing staircase. His hands were sore and his knee hurt and he was not looking forward to seeing Ben.

In the dingy kitchen, Old Mitch and Brian were washing up. Old Mitch was patiently telling Brian what to do, though they had washed up hundreds of times before. Tamar's dumpy little mother sat by the doorway. She wore a long black skirt and a headscarf. She tapped her fingers on her bag, clearly annoyed.

'Hullo,' said Beetle, 'waiting for Tamar?'

'Yes. They say not room in dressing-room. I must wait – out here.'

'It gets very hot in there,' said Old Mitch.

But Tamar's mother only sniffed. She stood up as Tamar came in and said something to her angrily in Kurdish.

Tamar answered her quietly and calmly, in a way that made it clear that she was not going to get into an argument.

Her mother began to tug at Tamar's sleeve.

'Mother, I am coming. Please don't pull me,' said Tamar in English. Her mother snapped back at her in Kurdish. Tamar gently released her arm and turned to Beetle.

'You did the lights all on your own, Beetle?'

'Yep.'

'It was good. I would not know the difference.'

'Oh, but I messed up all your last cues . . .'

'Really? I did not notice.'

'But it was awful . . .'

'Yeah, and thanks for blacking me out, man,' said Greg as he came in. He slapped Beetle on the back.

'Sorry, mate,' said Beetle. 'I don't know how that bit happened . . .'

'No sweat,' said Greg with a grin. 'Dunno how you do any of it – Q1, Q2, Q756 and all that.'

'Well, I couldn't do all those words like you

do,' said Beetle. 'And now I'm beginning to think I can't do the lighting either.'

Ben came into the kitchen with an empty mug and dropped it into the soapy water in the sink. It splashed Brian who flapped at him with a drying-up cloth. Ben put both his arms round him in a mock-wrestle and pretended to dunk him in the sink. Brian cackled loudly and elbowed Ben in the ribs. Ben couldn't be too angry then.

'Sorry, Ben,' said Beetle. 'I'm really sorry.'

'Oh you're here, are you?' said Ben. 'That was a fine mess you made up there.'

'I'm really, really sorry.'

Beetle couldn't think of anything else to say.

'Well,' said Ben, 'to be honest, Beetle, it wasn't all that bad. Pretty good, really, for your first time alone. I've known a lot worse.'

'I'm afraid – er, I'm afraid you don't know the half,' said Beetle, sitting down suddenly on an old wooden chair that wobbled beneath him.

Tamar knelt down beside him.

'But Beetle, you have blood on your jeans – and your hands, look at your hands . . .'

' 'S nothing,' said Beetle.

'OK, let's be having it,' said Ben. 'What's been going on up there?'

'Ben, I – there's a hole in the floor. Down the far end.'

'You've gone through the floor? Down at the end where you're not supposed to be? Beetle, what were thinking about? Why, for Chrissake?'

'There was this kid from the dancing class. I called you, Ben, but you didn't answer . . . honest, and I thought . . . I was afraid she'd . . .'

Beetle stumbled through an explanation of what had happened.

'I just didn't know what to do, so—'

'Beetle, you could have been killed,' said Ben in a voice tight with fury. 'You know that. You know how dangerous it is.'

'But what should I have done? You didn't answer . . .'

'OK, OK, yes. I'm sorry. There was an emergency down here too. I shouldn't have left the corner, but there was no one else.'

Ben turned to Old Mitch.

'Why wasn't the door locked, Mitch?'

'It was.'

'It can't have been,' said Beetle. 'I'm sure I heard her go back through the curtains and then the door slammed.'

Old Mitch hesitated. Beside him, Brian grinned,

and said 'slammed, slammed,' testing a beautiful new word.

'The key hangs up beside the door. I thought it was too high for the kids to reach, but maybe . . . I'd better check in the morning.'

'Yes,' said Ben, 'you better had, or someone's going to get killed, Mitch.'

The old man grunted, wiped his hands on a cloth, and led Brian away into the auditorium to tidy it up. Beetle felt quite sorry for him.

'And I'll have a word with Miss James to make sure the kids don't wander off,' said Ben. 'Look, Beetle, I can see you did the best you could, but you should have waited for me to come back.'

Beetle nodded, miserably.

'What about your hands,' said Tamar, who was still kneeling beside him, 'and your knee? Let me see, Beetle.'

'No, 's all right,' said Beetle. 'It's only splinters. And my knee's just grazed, I think.'

He examined his knee through the rip in his jeans.

'Yeah. No sweat.'

'Hey, man,' said Greg, 'your old lady will go mad about those.'

'Mum? Shan't tell her,' he said with a shrug. 'I can

take care of it. I'll cobble them together and shove them in the wash. I got to go to the laundrette in the morning. She'll never notice.'

Suddenly, Tamar's mother took his hands. She made a tutting noise.

'Must – wash,' she said.

'Yes,' said Tamar. 'They will go septic. You must get those splinters out.'

Ben took a first-aid box from a dusty shelf and began to tend Beetle's splinters. The stuff he put on stung – a lot. Greg was highly amused at the look on his face as Beetle bit his lips and tried not to say 'ouch' too loudly.

'Great mate you are,' said Beetle.

Ben picked away at a specially deep splinter with a needle.

'Tell me,' he said, 'which of the little girls was it up there?'

'Don't know her name. She was really little. I think she's the one who's always with Kiley.'

'Hmm.'

'It was while you were singing, Tamar. Did you see her up on the balcony, leaning over towards you?'

'No, I didn't, thank goodness,' said Tamar. 'I would be very worried to see a child up there alone

– it is too high up. But it's all just a big, dark, empty space from the stage.'

Her mother gave Tamar's arm another tug, more gently this time.

'I think – the boy is – OK now.'

'Yes,' said Tamar. 'We must go. My brother will be angry if he finds out I am out late.'

She glanced quickly at Beetle.

'It is later than usual. You know . . .'

Beetle nodded, remembering the two boys, but saying nothing.

'Greg, this looks like it's going to take a while. Why don't you go on? You can walk Tamar and her mum a little way.'

'Yeah?' said Greg, surprised.

'Yeah,' said Beetle. 'Why not?'

As Greg passed him, he muttered: 'Tell you why later.'

Greg gave a brief nod. Tamar said goodnight and the three of them left.

Old Mitch came back and started to hand Brian some cups and plates to stack away in the shabby, red-painted cupboard over the sink. Old Mitch looked at Beetle.

'Saw one of the dancing-class kiddies up on the balcony, did you?'

'Yes,' said Beetle.

'I'm sure the door was locked,' said Old Mitch. 'I thought the key was too high for kiddies to reach, but I must have been wrong.'

He hesitated, then turned away.

'Another little job for us, Brian. We'd better go up and have another look tomorrow.'

Brian grinned happily and clattered the cups.

At last, Ben finished digging about in Beetle's hands. They were red and sore but splinter-free. Ben screwed the top back on the bottle.

'Now look, young Beetle,' he said. 'I'm going to have to come on strong about this. You might have had a really bad accident up there. I shouldn't have let you up on the balcony on your own.'

Beetle opened his mouth to interrupt.

'Shut it,' said Ben. 'Let me finish. Now listen, that's the last time.'

'You mean on my own?'

'No, Beetle, I'm afraid I mean – at all.'

'But, Ben—'

'No. I'm sorry, Beetle. But you should never be up there. You're not insured. I should never have let you go in the first place.'

'Oh, Ben . . . Please . . . It'll never happen again. I won't ever leave the desk – and if Zak's there . . .

Honest, I won't move . . . only . . .'

'Sorry, Beetle. I'm sorry. But that's it. Listen, get your mum to look at those hands in the morning.'

'Eh? Oh sure,' said Beetle, giving them a hasty wipe on his jeans.

'Go on then, off you go,' said Ben, and, zipping up his jacket, he left.

Slowly, his hands stinging and his heart heavy, Beetle followed him. In the hallway, Zak was just coming downstairs from turning off the mains. Beetle started to tell him the whole sorry story as they left.

Behind them, Old Mitch locked the main doors. He went back into The Hall and stood for some time looking up at the deep shadows on the balcony. Then he shook his head, turned off all the lights and left by the side entrance.

And Beetle, deeply dejected and still talking to Zak under a street light, did not see the strange, troubled look on Old Mitch's face as he trudged off between the empty market barrows down the street.

Chapter 5

Greg stood in the poky little dressing-room. The lights round the dressing-tables were out but he didn't notice how dingy and scruffy the place looked – this was where he felt at home. He hung up the clean shirt his nan had just ironed for him. He brushed off the satin lapels of his costume and checked that his shoes were high-gloss polished ready for the evening's full dress rehearsal of 'your own – your very own' community concert.

Satisfied that he would be looking his best, he turned to go out and find Beetle. He wanted to know what had happened after he left with Tamar and her mother last night, and why Beetle wanted him to see her home. He opened the door and stopped. Somewhere out in The Hall there was an almighty row going on.

'Don't give me that crap, Mitch.'

Ben's voice – and he was angry.

'Well, Mr Starkey, the key was in its place like I said, much too high for any kid to reach, even Beetle, and there's nothing to stand on up there.'

'Are you saying Beetle made the story up? Because that's the only other explanation.'

'No, I'm not. You know what I'm saying. Young Beetle must have seen—'

'Mitch – do you take me for an idiot? Beetle must have gone down to the end of the balcony for – for, I don't know, for kicks, I suppose. And when he fell through, he made up the story of the dancing-class kid to get him out of trouble.'

Greg almost ran out to protest. Beetle might do a lot of things, but not that – but Old Mitch got in first.

'Beetle wouldn't do that, Mr Starkey, you know he wouldn't. Whatever else, he's never been a liar.'

There was a short silence, then Old Mitch went on.

'Anyway, why should he choose that story? Why say he saw a little girl holding out her arms to someone down on the stage? How would he know about that?'

'I don't know, Mitch. I just don't know. Coincidence maybe.'

Old Mitch grunted.

'They say it means trouble . . . they say it's a

warning . . . that she comes to—'

'That's enough. The last thing we need is wild rumours around with a show going on with kids in it. So just keep it quiet, will you?'

Old Mitch nodded.

'Well, whatever happened – and I still think if it wasn't a dancing-class kid up there it must have been Beetle messing about,' said Ben,' so it's down to one of you. Anyway, is the door safe now?'

'Of course it is. I told you, it was locked before. But now I've taken the key away, and we've fitted bolts top and bottom on the balcony side, haven't we, Brian?'

There was a sound that could have been 'yes, yes, yes,' and a giggle. Brian had enjoyed helping to screw bolts into the door. Brian enjoyed everything.

Greg waited till he heard Ben disappear to his office up the back stairs and Old Mitch and Brian were occupied in the workroom. He slipped out. But as he passed the workroom door, he heard Brian cackling away happily, singing 'ghostie, weeeeee, ghostie, weeeeee,' till Old Mitch shut him up by giving him something to hammer.

Ghostie . . . ghost. Is that what Old Mitch thought Beetle had seen? But no one knew the real story of the ghost – if there was one. It was just a wild sort of rumour that changed with every telling – werewolves in the basement, skeletons behind the door on the landing, a weeping woman in the wings, bats in the belfry. All nonsense. And no one had mentioned anything weird, let alone a little girl, up on the balcony. But if anyone knew the true story it would be Old Mitch . . .

Greg went up the draughty passage to the front door. At the bottom of the stairs to the balcony, he paused. He had never been up there. If he went to look, he would have a much better idea of what Beetle was on about – and if Beetle could go up there alone, so could he.

He looked round. No one was about. He started upwards, his trainers making the faintest of sounds in the dim light. He peered upwards. The railing seemed to go up for ever, up to the dirty skylight at the top that cast deep shadows into the corners where the cobwebs lurked. Greg swallowed. It was so quiet. If only he could hear Brian hammering . . . To keep his courage up, he started to take the stairs two at a time. At the bend by the leaning door, he stopped to get his breath. As he paused, the door seemed to loom towards him. It creaked. Surely the handle was turning slowly. He stepped back, holding his breath. The door creaked again, but nothing else happened. He took a step forward. The handle definitely moved. Greg did not wait. He hurled himself down the stairs, along the passage and out into the street.

He pulled himself together. He wasn't really scared, of course. It was just that there would have been trouble if he'd been caught up there alone – better to leave it till he could go up with Beetle or Zak or someone. It was early closing day and the street was empty of market stalls, but he set off with a jaunty step towards the park, where he installed himself high up on the parapet of the park gates – also banned, but a painless way of restoring his battered ego. Beetle always came back from the laundrette that way on Saturdays about this time.

Half an hour later, he was still waiting for Beetle when Kiley and her gran appeared. Kiley was holding her gran's hand, swinging her arm backwards and forwards as she skipped along, talking at the top of her voice.

'. . . and he made a terrible muddle, and it turned all the lights off. It was awful.'

Her gran did not reply, but nodded absently.

'He did. You should have been there. And Ben shouted at him through that microphone thing. We could all hear. And it went on for hours and hours.'

'Oh no it didn't, Kiley Smith, you're telling porkies again.'

Greg leaped off the parapet and Kiley let out a yell. Her gran came to with a start.

'Whatever's the matter, love?'

'He frightened me. He made me jump.'

She managed to put a little sob into her voice. Her gran put an arm round her.

'Come off it, Kiley,' said Greg. 'Take more than that to scare you, I know. And you were, you were telling big fat porkies. The lights weren't out for hours and hours. Not even minutes and minutes.'

'Well it seemed like it, sitting there in the dark,' said Kiley. 'Anyway, he's not allowed to do the lights any more, so it must have been awful.'

'What do you mean?' said Greg.

'It's true. Ben said. Old Mitch just told my gran, didn't he, Gran?'

'Don't believe you,' said Greg.

'I'm afraid it's true, Greg,' said Kiley's gran. 'We met him on the way here. He said there'd been a bit of a – well, an accident.'

'I knew about that, but not that he'd been – Man, what'll he do? He'll be . . .'

'Serves him right. He's stupid. And he put the lights out. It just serves him right.'

'Now, Kiley,' said her gran, 'that's not kind, love. He'll be ever so upset.'

'Too right he will,' said Greg, turning to run and find him. But just then, a disconsolate Beetle came up the street, humping a huge, checked laundry bag stuffed full, and kicking an old Coke can. He looked up, saw Kiley, and gave an extra hefty kick so that the can ricocheted off the park railings and spun back into the kerb. He dropped the bag and jumped hard on the can, squashing it flat. Greg went over to him, his usually cheerful face creased up with concern.

'Is it true?'

'Yeah. I saw Zak last night. He says there's nothing he can do about it.'

'Even though you went to save that kid's life?'

'Nah. Zak says it wasn't so dangerous for her – she weighed less than me. I should've stayed put where I was. But it isn't that, it's because Ben realizes I shouldn't ever have been up there at all – not ever. It's all to do with insurance and that stuff.'

Beetle sat on the kerb with his head on his hands, and the laundry bag teetered over and drooped on his shoulder. Even Kiley was quiet at the sight of him. Greg crouched down and went to put an arm round his shoulders, but suddenly he felt that Beetle might shrug even him away. The set of his back seemed to put up barriers to anyone and everyone. Kiley's gran gave her hand a little tug.

'Come on, love, let's go on the swings like I promised.'

'But—'

'No, Kiley, we'll leave them alone. Beetle's a bit upset.'

She dragged Kiley off into the park, past the fountain with the fat boy and the fishes, past the ice-cream kiosk to the swings. Kiley's voice could be heard long after they disappeared, her high twin bunches with their corkscrew curls bobbing up and down as she panted along after her gran, protesting all the way.

'Thank goodness she's gone,' said Greg. 'She's all you need.'

'I don't care about her,' said Beetle. 'She's just a pain. This is serious. For real.'

Greg nodded.

'You must be gutted, man. I'm sorry... really, really sorry...'

Beetle gave a sigh.

'Well, can't do anything about it. Might as well come and watch the dress rehearsal tonight.'

'That'll kill you, man.'

'Nope,' said Beetle. 'I can sit and do all the lighting

cues in my head – so I can get Zak, if he screws up –
huh, *I* bet. No, but I can really watch you properly.
See how you go on. You know.'

They stood up.

'Maybe Ben'll change his mind.'

Beetle shook his head.

'He can't. He's not still mad at me. It's just – he
can't. Zak said.'

Beetle picked up his bag and started off down the
road. Greg hesitated, then, with a shuffling kind of
run, followed him.

'Listen . . . er . . . you know this kid, the one on the
balcony . . . Well, are you . . . you sure – I mean . . .
you sure you really saw her?'

'Don't you start, Greg. I'm fed up talking about
her. Nobody seems to believe me.'

'I do. I believe you, Beetle. It's just that . . .'

'Even Zak asked me if I'd made it all up to get me
out of trouble . . . I've had enough.'

And Beetle walked away quickly this time,
whacking the laundry bag viciously against the park
railings. Greg ran after him.

'Hey, man, don't . . . Stop. Listen. I didn't not
believe you. I just wanted to . . .'

But Beetle's back was unyielding. Greg dropped
behind and watched him. What to do? He couldn't

let him go like that. He dropped his head, took a deep breath and ran after him, overtaking him and standing in his path. Beetle tried to push past him, but Greg took him by the shoulders and looked hard into his eyes.

'Listen, will you?'

'No one believes—'

'Shut that. Listen. I do believe you. And I think Old Mitch believes you too.'

'Old Mitch?'

'I heard him and Ben. This morning. They didn't know I was there. And Old Mitch was trying to tell him what you saw and Ben wouldn't listen.'

'What are you on about?'

'Well, I didn't hear it all, but I think Old Mitch was trying to tell Ben that the little girl you saw was . . . was, well, the ghost.'

'Oh come on, Greg . . . don't be daft. Ghosts aren't like that, they're . . . they're . . .'

'Well? What?'

'I dunno. But not little girls dressed up in frilly frocks as real as – as bloomin' Kiley, for goodness' sake. And I heard the door slam. Ghosts go through doors, they don't slam them.'

Greg shook his head.

'Well I dunno either, but that's what Old Mitch was

trying to say. Maybe we should ask him.'

'And maybe pigs got wings. I'm fed up with the whole thing. Let's forget it. Listen, I need to tell you about Tamar and Zak and all that. That's really important. Come on, ugly.'

And Beetle slung the laundry bag on his back, gave Greg a friendly shove off the kerb, and they set off home together.

Chapter 6

'Going?' said Beetle. 'What do you mean, going?'

'Just what I say,' said Zak. 'This is my last gig here.'

Ben had allowed Beetle to watch the dress rehearsal from the wings. He had even handed Beetle his headphones and let him give Zak a couple of cues. The concert looked like being a huge success – the best ever, people were saying. True, the Wilson Brothers wouldn't get any laughs, but the steel band was a wow, Greg had found some wicked tongue-twisters for his introductions and the dancing-class kids, well, as Ben said, they'd bring tears to the eyes of their mums and dads in the audience, though he didn't explain quite what he meant by that. Kiley had slipped and fallen on her bottom but instead of standing still and yelling her head off as Beetle expected, she got up quickly and joined in as if nothing had happened and one of the Wilson Brothers had called her a 'proper little trouper'.

And we'll never hear the end of that, thought Beetle.

But now, The Hall empty again, he was hearing other things he didn't want to hear. Greg's mum was on nights at the hospital, so he had gone home with his big cuddly nan who'd dropped by to see that his costume was exactly right, and now Beetle was with Zak outside The Hall.

'But—' he said to Zak.

'Look,' said Zak. 'Sure, it's been great here, and um . . . I – I guess I'll miss you, Beetle, but for me the band is more important than The Hall, and this is our chance. We'll be on the road now, maybe for months, so I've got to call it a day here.'

'But . . .' said Beetle again, but couldn't go on. A big knot of tears gathered in his chest and threatened to spill upwards.

'When . . .'

He tried again, but couldn't get any further.

'Next week, but tonight's my last night here,' said Zak. 'We're starting in Sheffield. I'll send you a card.'

Zak looked down at Beetle's face.

'Hey, man,' he said. 'It's not the end of the world. I'll be back when the tour's over.'

'Yeah but . . .' said Beetle.

Zak sat down at the kerb, his bony knees bent up

like a stork's. He pulled Beetle down beside him. He smelled of a mixture of sweat, beer and a faint whiff of herbs and Beetle thought it was the most comforting smell in the world. And now, he was going away.

'Listen, Beetle – are you listening?'

Beetle nodded.

'Look, it's not as if you could come up and work the board with me any more. Is it?'

He nudged Beetle in the ribs with a pointed elbow. 'Is it?'

Beetle gave a watery smile and shook his head.

'So you won't be missing anything . . .'

'No?' said Beetle.

He lifted his head and looked at Zak. Zak dropped his gaze and picked at a thread on his jeans.

'Yeah, well . . . it's not for ever. We'll be back. It may not come to anything.'

'Yes it will,' said Beetle. 'You'll be a big star. Trust me. You will.'

'Think so?' Zak laughed. '*I* wish. Anyway, by that time you'll be big enough and ugly enough to come out on the road with us.'

'Honest?'

Beetle jumped up.

'D'you mean it? Can I really – come with you?'

'Hey, cool it, man,' said Zak.

He put out a hand and Beetle heaved him up. Then, seriously, he said:

'Sure. Why not? When you're just a bit older. You could come and learn to be a roadie – that's if we keep going. If. And it's a big if. Come on, I'll buy you a burger for old times' sake.'

As they waited in the queue at the burger bar, Beetle looked up at Zak, a question turning over in his mind. He wasn't sure he wanted the answer but it wouldn't go away.

'Za-a-ak,' he said.

'Now what? No, you can't have two.'

Beetle grinned and glanced away, jingling the key chain in his pocket.

'No, it's not that. It's . . . it's . . . you know the little kid I saw . . . up on the balcony.'

'Oh not that again.'

'No, listen. Greg says that Old Mitch said to Ben . . .'

'Wait a minute, who said what?'

'Zak, is there a ghost in The Hall?'

'Oh, Beetle, not that old crap again.'

'Greg heard Old Mitch and Ben talking. He thinks Old Mitch said that the little kid I saw was the ghost, the ghost of The Hall.'

They wandered out into the street, dropping chips into their mouths, talking with their mouths full.

'First I've heard of it.'

But there was something odd in the way Zak spoke and when Beetle looked at him, his head was turned away.

'Honest?'

Zak was having trouble with the hot chips.

'Zak?'

Zak mumbled. Before he could reply a voice from the other side of the street called out:

'Out with your boyfriend then, sweetie?'

The voice was strident and full of venom.

Zak wheeled round. He bunched his parcel of food into a tight ball and shoved it at Beetle.

'Hold that!'

One of the two boys who had taunted Tamar was laughing at them, keeping pace with them along the opposite pavement. His hands were shoved into his shiny jacket, his ears seemed to stick out on either side of his shaved head and even from this distance his teeth looked yellow and dirty from fags and worse. Zak started to run across the street towards him, but suddenly, from a doorway, the second boy appeared and put a foot out, tripping Zak and sending him sprawling into the gutter. He hit his head on the kerb and lay still. Beetle raced across to him. The two boys ran off, shrieking with laughter.

'That's right, nancy boy! Better look after your *friend* then! Oops a daisy, darlin'!'

Beetle swore at them as they went, but they were too busy congratulating themselves on their own wit to bother. He knelt beside Zak, terrified of what he would find, but Zak was blinking and groaning, beginning to sit up, feeling his head. Hastily, he pushed Beetle to one side and threw up into the gutter.

'Bastards!' he muttered, as he wiped his mouth on a grey old handkerchief he kept to dry his face during a gig. Beetle helped him to his feet.

'I'll get them for that,' he said as Zak explored the lump that was already growing like an egg on his forehead.

'You will not,' said Zak. 'You'll leave them alone.'

'Me and Greg could take 'em.'

'No. I mean it. Just keep – keep an eye on Tamar. All the time. When there's a rehearsal or a show, try and find out if she's coming without her mum, and if she is, make sure you meet her – with Greg if you can. Make it look like coincidence. But don't let her alone with those two around. And if there's any trouble, don't go in on your own or with Greg. Just tell Ben.'

'OK.'

'And Beetle. Forget about ghosts, huh? Anyway, you can't go up on the balcony now, so – just forget about it.'

'Well . . .'

Zak gave him a friendly shove.

'Go on, there's more important things to think about now.'

More important than lighting shows? Beetle looked at him. He must mean his new life with Ellsteef, out on the road, playing his music, forgetting The Hall and the lighting board and the great times they had had.

'Oi!' said Zak. 'I mean looking out for Tamar. I'm relying on you. Go on now, get off home. It's late. Your mum'll be worried after you.'

'Don't think so,' said Beetle. 'I've told you before, she never worries after me. She doesn't have to. I can take care of myself – and Tamar.'

He grinned sympathetically at Zak who was wagging his head with a grimace as he remembered the lump.

'You OK?'

'I'll live.'

They walked together to the doorway of the tower block where Beetle lived. He peered up at the ninth floor. There were no lights on, but he had the key.

'See you then, mate.'

'Yeah. See you.'

They shook hands, high five, fist and palms. Zak turned and walked away. Beetle watched him for a moment and then started to leg it up the endless stairs. The lift was probably out of order yet again, and anyway it would be filthy and stinking, too horrible for even Beetle to think of using.

The eerily-lit staircase seemed to hold a multitude of threats. It seemed to hide not ghosts, but things and people that meant terrible harm. The balcony in The Hall seemed far away, like a beautiful dream he had to wake up from. Reality was this place and getting up to the ninth floor unscathed in the dark.

He started to hurry, setting an empty tin rattling through the railing and down to the concrete floor below. Swearing under his breath, he stopped and listened.

Ahead of him he heard heavy footsteps trudging upwards. He slowed down and started to creep. No point asking for trouble. But slow as he was, he was gaining on whoever it was ahead.

And then the footsteps stopped. Outside, a sudden wind moaned around the tower blocks. Old newspapers rustled round the tin rolling and clattering at the bottom of the stairwell. Then there was silence. But someone was waiting up ahead. Scarcely breathing, Beetle peered upwards but he could see nothing. Then, pulling back on the handrail, he pushed off and jumped, clawing the air. He grabbed the rail overhead and with a huge effort pulled himself up till he could just see the floor above. Two feet were pressed against the wall away from him, ready to spring – or run.

He knew those feet. He flopped down from the rail with a grunt of laughter and raced up the stairs.

'It's OK, it's only me! Beetle!'

'Oh Lor',' said Kiley's gran, putting her hand to her chest. 'Thank heavens. I thought it was – well, I don't know quite, but someone nasty . . .'

'Sorry,' said Beetle. 'Didn't mean to scare you. But I didn't know who you were either and you . . .'

'I scared you?'

'Oh no . . . well – a bit.'

Kiley's gran was shaking. Beetle put a hand under her elbow.

'Come on. I'll see you in.'

'You're not a bad lad at heart, Beetle.'

'Who says I was?'

He looked up at her under his eyelids with a grin.

'You know what I mean,' she said.

Beetle knew exactly what she meant. Things he'd done, ages ago or so it seemed, but that he'd rather not think about too much now.

At her front door on the sixth floor, he took her keys, opened the door and stretched out a hand to feel for the light. He froze.

She was there. The little girl from The Hall was sitting on the back of a chair, her white dress gleaming in the half-light. Great dead eyes seemed to stare past him as she toppled forward slowly and fell, her long lank hair swinging out towards him. He fumbled about for the light switch but behind him, Kiley's gran flicked it on. She went into the room, picked up the doll, shook out its frilled Victorian dress and put it down on the seat of the chair.

'Silly place to leave her,' she said. 'Might have got broken. She was my gran's. Ever so old. Pretty, isn't she? Come on in, love.'

With a deep breath and feeling rather stupid, Beetle edged into the room and closed the door. The little flat was stuffed full of ornaments, just like her stall. Cups and saucers with fancy handles and gold rims were stacked in a glass-fronted cupboard and pink and white statues of shepherds and shepherdesses also trimmed with gold stood on every available space. By the gas fire a huge orange vase burgeoned with paper poppies, bright red with black-eyed centres.

'Like a cup of tea, love, or will your mum be waiting for you?'

'Shouldn't think so. Light wasn't on upstairs. You been to Bingo?'

'Mmm. Didn't win anything.'

She glanced up.

'Your mum wasn't there.'

'No? Oh well. Went to the pub after work, I expect . . . I'll put the kettle on. You're still shaking a bit.'

So was he, just a little, but he wasn't going to say.

'I suppose it's daft to go out at night when you're getting on a bit, like me. But I'm not going to let those . . . those . . .'

Kiley's gran cast a look at Beetle and decided against the word that was really in her mind.

'. . . those evil little devils that live round here frighten me off from going out when and where I want. I'm glad you're not in with that lot, Beetle.'

Beetle busied himself with the kettle and some tea bags. He didn't answer. There was a time when he might have been – almost was – one of those 'evil little devils', but The Hall and Zak and the lighting had become more important somehow. Well, Zak was going now and it looked like it would be a long time before he'd be allowed up on the balcony again, but he'd wait . . . he'd wait . . . He turned off the tap with a wrench.

Kiley's gran moved the doll to one side, eased herself heavily into the big armchair beside it and pulled off her shoes. She gave a grunt as they plopped to the floor. All her spryness and life seemed drained away. Beetle moved a china poodle covered in white curlicues on the table at her side and put a cup of tea on the beer mat it had been standing on.

'Ta, dear, lovely,' she said. 'You been at the rehearsal?'

'I watched from the wings.'

'So they didn't let you do the lighting with Zak?'

Beetle shook his head and poked a toe at the flowers on the carpet.

'Oh, I see.'

'No you don't,' said Beetle quickly. 'I never did anything wrong. It's the insurance.'

'The what?'

Kiley's gran gave a little laugh as she answered. She was beginning to be her old self as she sipped her tea.

'They say I'm not allowed up there, it isn't safe.'

'I'm not surprised. Even when I was young it was dark and dusty up there. Hardly ever used. But now, Old Mitch says you can go through the floor. So they've stopped you going up then, have they? Well – just as well, I reckon.'

'Why?'

'Oh nothing . . . just dangerous.'

'Old Mitch says . . .'

'Yes?'

'He says that there's a gho—'

'Oh he does, does he? Well, don't you take any notice of that, young Beetle. And don't go spreading stories. I don't want Kiley – or any of the kids from the dancing class – frightened with all that rubbish. D'you hear?'

'So it's not true. I said it wasn't. I told Greg – if there's a ghost in that place it's behind that door on the front stairs up to the balcony. Anyway, whoever heard of a ghost being a little girl, for goodness' sake?'

'A little girl?'

Kiley's gran put down her tea. Beetle looked at her but suddenly she seemed to be having trouble with the buttons on her coat.

'A little girl, did you say? Where?'

'Up on the balcony, leaning over. Greg heard Old Mitch say—'

73

'You tell Greg not to believe everything he hears, specially round there at The Hall,' said Kiley's gran.

She heaved herself up and the doll rolled over and collapsed across the chair. As she pulled off her coat, Kiley's gran smothered a yawn. Beetle frowned. He wasn't sure it was a real yawn. She hadn't finished her tea either, and now he had the feeling she wanted him to leave.

'I'm getting a bit tired, love. Time to climb the wooden hill . . .'

She gave a little laugh.

'As if I hadn't climbed far enough already. Thanks ever so much for seeing me in and making the tea and everything. Like I said, you're not a bad lad.'

She patted him on the shoulder, shuffled over to the door in her stockinged feet and opened it a crack. She peered down the landing.

'All clear,' she said. 'No one about down here, anyway. You hurry on up, love. And listen, no more stories about ghoulies and ghosties and things that go bump in the night. There's enough real things that do that round here. Just – just you take care, that's all.'

She opened the door a little wider to let Beetle through. He glanced back at the doll lying on the chair, staring vacantly into space. He wanted to ask what he should take care of, but Kiley's gran was already double-locking the door and shooting the bolts behind him.

Chapter 7

'One's called Pasty White – kind of nickname, I guess.'

'Suits him, he's like a great white slug.'

'And the other's called Nick something or other, I can't remember. It's a long name. My brother knows it.'

'Doesn't matter, Nick Spitz'll do. He's always at it. Hawking and spitting. Haven't you seen him? Ugh! Gross.'

Beetle laughed.

They sat on the bottom step of the staircase in The Hall. A crowd of little girls came in through the front doors, bringing a gust of air to sweeten the stuffy smell from the kitchen. Among them was Kiley, holding her mum's hand. She swept past the boys with her nose in the air, today's lime green tights sparkling. She spoilt the regal effect by stopping at the stairs to the basement to turn and make the ugliest face she could manage. Beetle and Greg retaliated in kind and they could hear her wailing all the way down the stairs that 'those awful boys had made faces at her'. Fortunately, her voice was soon muffled by the clip-clip of a dozen tap-shoed feet on the stone. Greg cast his eyes to heaven.

'How does anyone get to be that horrible?'

'Never mind all that,' said Beetle, 'we've got to do something about Tamar. How do we find out when she's coming here on her own?'

'Ask her,' said Greg. 'I mean – just ask her. Say to her Zak told us to look out for her when she's on her own. Zak didn't say not to tell her, did he?'

'Not really,' said Beetle, doubtfully. 'Not in so many words, but the whole point is – she wants to come here alone. Without her mum. Without anyone, I'd say. I think she'll tell us to get lost. I would.'

'Hmm.'

Another gaggle of little pony-tailed tap-dancettes burst into the hallway, followed by the pianist who gave them a glare over his glasses as usual.

'I've had enough of this,' said Greg. 'Can't get a bit of peace and quiet anywhere round here. The judo kids'll be in next.'

Beetle jerked his head upwards.

'We can go on up a bit,' he said, 'so long as we

don't go right up to the balcony.'

'In your dreams,' said Greg, staying put.

'Why not? Don't you care about Tamar?'

'It's not that . . . I . . .'

Greg gave a quick glance up the stairs.

'You're not scared, are you? I said you were, the other day . . .'

Hands in pockets, Greg scuffed at the bottom step, avoiding Beetle's eye. He started to say something then stopped. Beetle pulled him round to face him and gradually dragged from him the story of his little adventure up the stairs.

'The handle turned?'

'Yep.'

Greg was certain.

'Something in a cupboard sounds much more likely than little girls on the balcony,' said Beetle with something like relief. 'Come on, let's go and look.'

Greg held his ground, picking at a bit of loose paint on the wall.

'Chicken,' said Beetle. 'Well, I'm going up anyway.'

He started legging it up the stairs, making loud clucking noises, but at the first bend the silence seemed to descend like a mist and his voice died away to nothing. He went on, but slower and with less noise, till he reached the landing near the door.

Everything was still, nothing moved in the shadows, but suddenly, he was sure the door creaked. He swallowed. Kicking the door and running wouldn't tell him what was inside the cupboard; besides, his legs didn't seem to be in the mood for kicking, they seemed to want to stand still or even go back downstairs.

He edged a little closer. Slowly the handle turned. The skin on the back of his neck began to creep. He took another tiny step. Another creak and the handle turned again.

'Told you.'

Beetle nearly leaped out of his skin. He spun round, almost knocking Greg down the stairs.

'Hey, man, watch it.'

'Don't you ever, ever creep up on me like that again.'

Beetle was white and shaking.

'I thought you'd hear me coming up the stairs.'

'Well, I didn't. And I left you shivering in your shoes down there.'

'You knew I'd come.'

'No, I didn't.'

'Oh yes—'

This looked like turning into a Kiley kind of argument. Beetle blew out a breath.

'Pffffff. Well anyway, we'll have scared off any spooks that might have been thinking of taking a peek out here.'

Greg moved up beside him, then grabbed his arm.

'No we haven't,' he said. 'Look.'

Sure enough, the handle had turned again.

'But it keeps turning,' said Beetle, 'and not opening.'

He went a little nearer.

'It's us,' he said. 'We're making it turn.'

He waved an arm.

'It's our reflection. It makes it look as if the handle moves. Look.'

And he waved his arm again.

'But why's the handle so shiny? There's nothing else up here looks clean and polished like that. Look at it.'

Swathes of black dust settled in crevices on the walls and the exit light glass was grimy and cracked.

'The handles to the balcony doors do,' said Beetle. 'They're brass too. Just the kind of thing Brian likes to polish.'

Greg stepped forward.

'Let's have a look inside,' he said.

'Gone all brave now, have you?' said Beetle, with a grin. 'But we don't know if Brian ever *looks inside* the cupboard, do we? He might just come up and polish the handles. There might still be skeletons inside. Anyway, I bet it's locked.'

Greg paused, then leaned forward, jerked at the handle, heaved and staggered backwards, almost toppling down the stairs. He hung on to the rail just in time. The door flew open.

Bones!

Long white bones topped with a hank of matted grey hair loomed towards them, slowly at first, then gaining momentum, reaching out for them. With a yell, they turned to run, but the clatter and thud behind them told them that this was no skeleton, no ghost, but a cupboard full of brooms and mops that had tumbled out with the force of the opening door. With another yell, this time of laughter, Beetle and Greg clung to each other, then started to pick up the things that had fallen. Greg took the mop and, turning it into a monster puppet, made it dance about, making ghoulish noises, shaking its manky grey locks like a fiend from the underworld. Beetle choked back his laughter.

'Shut up! Shut up! They'll hear us from downstairs and they'll never believe we weren't going up to the balcony . . . Greg . . . shut it, will you?'

But Greg went on bouncing about with the mop,

butting Beetle in the face and the stomach, making screeching noises, till Beetle laughed in spite of himself. But wait . . . someone was hurrying up the stairs. Brisk footsteps were coming up at a trot. They dropped everything and without thinking, raced upstairs. There was nowhere to hide, except inside the balcony doors. In a panic, they slipped through and up the steps behind the lighting desk. They waited. In the dark, they could hear the faint sounds from below of the mops and brooms being put back in the cupboard. Then the door slammed. Which way would the footsteps go? They prayed silently for them to go down again. But nothing happened. The feet apparently stayed where they were.

The plop, plop of water somewhere close at hand, the lonely tick of the meter for the lighting rig, even their own breathing seemed magnified in the silence of the balcony. But someone was still down there. What was whoever it was doing, keeping so quiet? Listening? For them?

They waited, their eyes getting used to the dark. The exit lights were out, and only thin pencils of light came through the scratches on the paint on the windows. There was a grey chill over everything. Greg edged closer to Beetle. He peered out across the vast space over the auditorium, then whispered:

'Wh . . . where . . . ?'

Beetle smacked a finger to his lips, mouthing 'ssssh'. He pointed away to his right, towards the end of the balcony, shrouded in darkness, where the little girl had been and where there was now a large hole in the floor with some of his knee sticking to the edge.

Greg nodded and was about to say something else, when they heard footsteps tapping up the stairs outside. They flattened themselves into the shadows. Beetle suddenly felt a surge of hope that it might be Zak. If so, they might get away with being up here, but he wore Docs and they would make more noise than this. They waited, but the doors didn't open. Someone outside was thumping against them rhythmically. There was a flapping sound and then a tuneless singing, followed by a whistle that was no whistle but a kind of blowing with a lot of spit.

Beetle gave a yelp of laughter, dashed down the steps and out through the doors, nearly pushing over the person outside. Greg followed him, puzzled, but not wanting to be left alone on the balcony.

Outside, on the stone landing, stood Brian, duster in one hand, tin of Brasso in the other. He was brushing some Brasso from his old blue jumper, spilt when Beetle burst through the door. He muttered.

'Sorry, sorry!' said Beetle. 'Here. Come here.'

He grabbed the duster and wiped Brian's jumper energetically. The Brasso gradually merged with all the other stains on his front. He grabbed the duster back, gave Beetle a push and returned to polishing the door handles with great vigour. He had obviously taken the hump.

'Brian!'

A voice called from below. It reverberated round the stairwell.

'You finished yet? Cuppa tea time!'

Brian's mood changed abruptly and he grinned, showing grubby crooked teeth and dribbling a little.

'Tea,' he said. 'Tea, tea, hee.'

'That's right,' said Beetle. 'Come on. We'll give you a hand to put this away,' and he and Greg escorted Brian to the cupboard on the stairs where Brian insisted on putting things away in immaculate rows and straightening the already tidy brooms and mops. Meanwhile Old Mitch was toiling up the stairs behind them.

'Come on, Brian, me old love, I can hear your tea getting cold from here.'

Brian grinned and said 'Tea, tea, hee,' some more. Old Mitch put an arm round his shoulders to encourage him down the stairs, but then looked back.

'Oi. What are you two doing up here? What are you up to now?'

'Er . . .' said Beetle, but Brian interrupted.

'Jump, jump, jump,' he said, looking cross. He gave his shoulders a little twitch and jumped up and down heavily.

'What?'

Beetle looked guilty.

'Made you jump, did they? Have you two been messing about with Brian? Listen, I won't have that – that's not right.'

'No,' said Greg. 'Honest.'

'Well, only a little bit – it was a kind of accident – we didn't mean to. And I cleaned up his jumper for him, where he spilled the polish, didn't I, Brian? Honest, we didn't mean to frighten him. We wouldn't.'

'Huh,' said Old Mitch. 'Better not. And you haven't been up on the balcony, have you?'

'Not really,' said Beetle. 'Well, only just inside the doors, but we didn't know who Brian was and we were by the cupboard and we heard . . . and we ran . . . and . . .'

'Oh for goodness' sake,' said Old Mitch. 'Forget it, but just don't go up there at all – ever – will you?

D'you understand? Never. I thought you'd learned your lesson, Beetle. Well, if I catch you up there again . . . There's been enough trouble already. Just let Ben Starkey catch you, that's all.'

'I know,' said Beetle, looking crestfallen.

'Oh, come on down and have a cup of tea,' said Old Mitch. 'You can give me a hand with the art class washing up.'

'Oh great,' said Greg under his breath. Beetle kicked him on the ankle and they went down into the fug of the kitchen, where Brian's tea stood on the battered draining board, fast growing a thin, wrinkly skin. He grabbed it and nursed it to him.

'You can't drink that,' said Old Mitch, taking it away and pouring it down the sink. 'Put the kettle on and we'll start again.'

He reached into a cupboard and fetched out a packet of Rich Tea biscuits. Brian clapped his hands in glee and grabbed them. He fumbled at the wrapping, and Old Mitch gently took them from him, opened them neatly, and gave him first pick.

'What, er – what are you boys so interested in up there, anyway?' said Old Mitch, busying himself with the teapot.

'Oh,' said Beetle, 'nothing really. We just—'

'Yes, we are,' said Greg, crunching his biscuit. 'It's

all these stories about ghosts.'

'Ghosties . . . weeeee . . .' said Brian, spraying crumbs everywhere.

Old Mitch gave him a look.

'What stories?' he said, in a casual way.

'You know,' said Greg, 'werewolves in the basement, skeletons in the cupboard. So we went up to have a look – in the cupboard.'

Old Mitch gave a little smile.

'And are there any?'

'Course not,' said Greg. 'Just a lot of old mops and brooms.'

Beetle suddenly decided that they'd had enough beating about the bush. He settled himself on a stool and looked straight at Old Mitch, trying to catch his eye, but he was busy pouring the tea.

'It's more than that, Mitch,' he said. 'It's more than stories – we know there's nothing in the cupboard, but what about – what about the little girl . . . the little girl I saw on the balcony?'

'Yes?' said Old Mitch, handing him a mug but still not meeting his eye. 'One of the dancing-class kiddies, wasn't it?'

'But the door was locked, wasn't it Mitch?'

'It is now.'

'It was before. You said. You said it to Ben.'

'She must have got the key. It was hanging up. Kids are into everything these days, can't leave anything. I wouldn't put anything past them. Nor past you, either.'

'I didn't make up the story, if that's what you mean.'

'Didn't say you did,' said Old Mitch, and he gave Brian another biscuit.

'Listen,' said Beetle, 'I saw that kid, and I'm beginning to think—' but just then the art class emerged from the side room, bringing trays of dirty cups and saucers. They banged them down on the draining board and reached out to raid the Rich Tea packet.

'Oh no you don't,' said Old Mitch and spirited them away. The art class gathered in the tiny kitchen, chattering like magpies and fingering everything with paint-covered hands.

'Right. That's it,' said Old Mitch. 'Go on, outside, shove off all of you.' And he and Brian began to shoo everyone out of the door. 'And you two.'

'But we were going to help you—'

'Brian and me'll manage. Go on, off you go. Making the place untidy.'

He paused.

'And er . . . just, just . . . well, take care, eh?'

And without further ado, Old Mitch firmly propelled them outside and closed the kitchen door.

'Just as we were beginning to get somewhere,' said Beetle.

'You reckon?' said Greg. 'I don't think he was giving anything away. But I tell you what, I think he knows something.'

'Yes,' said Beetle, 'you're right. And I wonder why everyone's on at me to "take care" all of a sudden. First Kiley's gran and now Old Mitch. They've never said anything like that before ... before I saw the girl up there. Listen. I think Kiley's gran knows something too – but they're neither of them telling. Neither of them. They're not saying one word – but they know. Trust me. They know.'

Chapter 8

The 'new Zak' wore an old green boiler suit. He wore it over old flannel trousers, a shirt with a frayed collar and a grey woolly jumper. His pointed leather shoes were cracked and his stomach bulged. His hair was thin and going grey and was plastered down flat to his head with little rat's tails sticking out just above his collar. Beetle eyed him with suspicion. He knew there was no chance of going up to the balcony ever again, but he might, he just might have been allowed to help round the electrics in The Hall itself, if the new techie had been friendly. If. Friendly was not the word that came to mind when you looked at the stony, mud-coloured eyes of Mr Daniels. Ben said that any attempt to call him by his first name, whatever it was, or 'Danny' or even 'Mr D', had apparently been met with 'Mr Daniels will do, thank you'.

Beetle's face when he met Mr Daniels made

Ben laugh. He put a hand on Beetle's shoulder and murmured in his ear:

'Give it a chance, Beetle. It's not for ever. Give it a chance.'

Mr Daniels had offered Beetle a flabby hand when introduced. Now he started to plod up the stairs to the balcony.

'He'll go through the floor,' said Beetle in horror.

'Zak's shown him exactly where it's safest to tread,' said Ben. 'Don't worry. Nothing needs rigging for this show now, so he'll only need to stick to the area by the board, and it's safe enough there. And by the time things need changing, either we'll have someone new and permanent and under seventeen stone or, well, Zak may be back. You never know.'

Beetle brightened.

'Think so?'

'Don't count on it. I mean, we all hope the band gets really big – but it's chancy out there, you know.'

Beetle nodded, torn between wishing hard for Zak and Ellsteef to go racing up the charts and wishing hard for Zak to come back to The Hall and for things to be the way they were.

At least Ben had told Mr Daniels that Beetle could be, would be, a great help to him, given half a chance, even if he wasn't allowed up on the balcony. He could re-aim lamps in the auditorium and on stage. He could cut gels. He could wire a switch. He could tape down cables. Mr Daniels had grunted, but had seemed unimpressed.

As Ben went up to his office, he turned.

'Hey, Beetle. Be careful what you say about our Mr Daniels. He's Old Mitch's brother-in-law – and he's doing us a good turn.'

He whistled loudly as he went upstairs.

Beetle banged out through the front doors into the market, to see Greg coming towards him. Hands in pockets, shoulders hunched up to his ears, Beetle did a kind of trundling gallop to meet him.

'What's up with you, man?'

'Nothing. Well . . . I just met the new Zak. Huh. New Zak. I *don't* think.'

'Gruesome?'

'Trust me. About as gruesome as you can get.'

'Now then, young Beetle.'

Kiley's gran was sitting on an upturned crate next to her stall. Her pink fluffy cardigan was buttoned up to her chin and she sipped coffee from a polystyrene cup.

'Just you give him a chance.'

'That's what Ben said.'

'I should think so. Just because he's not so young

and hasn't got half the jeweller's shop in his ear, doesn't mean he doesn't know his job. I'll have you know Fred Daniels was stage manager of a big West End theatre for years. It's very good of him to come out of retirement to help out.'

'Oh,' said Beetle.

'Yes. Oh,' said Kiley's gran. 'So you mind you show him a bit of respect, my lad. He's not likely to disappear at a moment's notice, at any rate. Not like some flighty people I could mention.'

Beetle looked fierce.

'Zak's not flighty, so don't say he is.'

Kiley's gran raised her eyebrows and opened her mouth to speak but changed her mind and sniffed instead. Then she smiled.

'Oh well,' she said, 'daresay you're right. But just the same, young Beetle, Fred Daniels could teach you a thing or two, if you go about him the right way.'

'What's the right way?'

'That's for me to know and you to find out,' said Kiley's gran, wagging a finger. She returned to her coffee and swivelled round with her back to them to speak to a customer.

Greg shrugged.

'Maybe he won't be too bad then.'

'Huh. In your dreams.'

'Maybe you should give him a chance, man.'

'Oh, not you too. Anyway, you haven't seen him, so give it a rest, will you?'

Greg gave him a look. 'Forget it,' he said. 'There's other more important things.'

'Like?'

'Like Tamar. She's coming to the rehearsal on her own. She told my brother.'

'Your brother seems to know everything.'

'Hey, don't be like that, man. Just because—'

Greg stopped himself. He tried a grin, instead.

'Hey, I guess my brother gets around, huh? Anyway, he told me Tamar is really scared.'

'Then why doesn't she come to rehearsal with her mum, then, like she used to?'

'What's up with you? Anyway, it's not just them she's afraid of – Pasty White and his mate. My brother says it's *her* brother she's scared of most.'

'Her brother? Why?'

'He's, like, he's head of the family now. Her dad died and now it's her brother says what's what. Even her mother has to do what he says. And he doesn't like Tamar singing, not in public, you know. So she sneaks out. Her mum knows, of course. She doesn't mind, I think maybe she quite likes it, but she just gets the jitters in case big brother finds out. Tamar'd be kept home, even from school, if he did, and she'll be coming up seventeen fairly soon.'

'That's out of order.'

'Too right, man. But my brother says that's what it's like for lots of the Kurdish people round here. I think it's to do with their religion. They're Muslim. I guess it's what they're used to.'

'Yeah, maybe, but then how come her brother doesn't find out?'

'He doesn't live round here. He's married and lives up in Hackney somewhere. But he still keeps a watch on them. Her little brother's still at home. He doesn't say anything, because he doesn't like being bossed by his big brother either.'

'Like you, you mean,' said Beetle, with the glimmer of a smile.

'Huh. Just let him try. Anyway, between them, they all manage to keep her singing a secret. That's why she's just called "Tamar" on the programme. It's not her real name, it's not even Kurdish. "Tamar" could be anyone. But now she wants to come to The Hall on her own to rehearsals, her mum's really worried. I mean, she'll be for it if anything happens to Tamar and he finds out.'

'Well, we'll just have to take care of it. Five o'clock, you said.'

He looked up at the huge old clock hanging sideways from a metal pole high up on the crumbling yellow bricks of The Hall. Ben took great pride in making sure it was always exactly right with Big Ben.

'Hey, it's nearly that now. Let's go.'

They dodged through the market and up a side street towards Ransome House, a towering cement block a little way away. Tamar lived above a small shop just beside it. The shop had a grille over the door and metal shutters covered in graffiti that looked very bright and cheerful until you read what it said. The Kurdish owners of the shop had long since been forced to move away by people who hated them because they believed they were 'different', but Tamar and her mother and younger brother stayed in the little flat because there was nowhere else to go.

Beetle and Greg hung about outside a shop selling TV sets round the corner from the flat, out of sight. In the window, coloured images flickered and changed soundlessly. Beetle and Greg took turns to peer round the corner every now again. Just as Greg leaned out, Beetle gasped.

'What is it?'

'It's her . . .' said Beetle, his eyes glued to a screen

at the top of the window. 'Look, it's her . . .'

'Who?'

Greg pulled back to squint up at the screen.

'The kid . . . the little girl . . . the one on the balcony.'

'Don't be daft, it can't be.'

'There was a kind of snowstorm, you know, like before you put in a video, and then . . . she had great big eyes, sort of – afraid, just like her . . . and a white dress. And she was reaching out, reaching out at me again, as if she would walk right out of the telly.'

'You're seeing things, man,' said Greg. 'Well, she's not there now.'

'One minute she was there and then – she vanished,' said Beetle, 'just like before . . .'

'Look. You've just got her on the brain, that's all. No way can she . . . You're seeing things. Listen, we'll have missed Tamar at this rate. It's well gone five.'

Reluctantly, Beetle turned away from the screen to follow Greg. They started to hurry back through the jigsaw of streets to The Hall. Suddenly, ahead of them, they spotted Tamar, scurrying along, her head down, hugging the wall. They closed the gap between them as inconspicuously as they could. They needn't have worried. Tamar had let her veil drop either side of her face like the blinkers on a racehorse.

Suddenly, there they were.

Pasty White and Nick Spitz were lounging in the entrance to the amusement arcade at the bottom of the market, framed by multi-coloured, flashing lights. The ping and zing of the machines and the deafening sound of thumping music blared past their shaved heads. As they saw Tamar, they flicked their fags away and started towards her.

Without a word and seeming not to hurry, Beetle and Greg slid into position on either side of her. She caught her breath and faltered, for a moment uncertain who they were. Beetle locked his face into a grin, speaking between clenched teeth.

'Hi, Tamar. Just keep going. Those two heroes have spotted you.'

'They won't try anything with the three of us in broad daylight,' said Greg, looking casually into the supermarket window, but not pausing for an instant.

'Keep going. Nearly there.'

Trying not to speed up, they glued themselves to Tamar's side. Pasty White and Nick Spitz followed a little way behind. There were too many people about for real trouble, but the threat was unmistakable. As the three turned smartly into the doors of The Hall, the two lads set up a rhythmic chanting, beating their fists in the air. 'Turkish scum, Turkish scum, out, out, out!'

'Don't answer,' said Beetle, taking Tamar's elbow and guiding her in ahead of him. 'Greg, leave it!'

Too late. Greg had turned back and given them two fingers before Beetle could stop him. He grabbed Greg's T-shirt and hauled him inside. The doors swung backwards and forwards violently.

'Shouldn't have done that, you wazzo.'

'Why not? I feel better.'

'You won't. They'll be looking for you too, now.'

'What's new? They're always after anyone black, or – only that's not what they call it. That's life, round here. I can handle it.'

Tamar gave a little sob.

'Well, I can't – and it is all my fault.'

'Quit that,' said Beetle, but not unkindly. 'Like Zak said, you've got a right to walk down the streets just like any of us.'

'It's horrible.'

Tamar shivered. Greg took her shoulders and gave her a little shake.

'Hey, no sweat. Beetle and me can handle those two. We promised Zak we'd keep an eye on you, and we will.'

'Zak?'

'Yeah. Last thing he said before he went.'

Tamar went pink under the honey-brown of her skin and twisted her veil.

'That – that was very kind of him. He is a kind man, I think.'

Beetle grinned and glanced at Greg from the corner of his eye.

'Yeah, well . . . come on, you've got a rehearsal to do. Last one before the final dress and there's a new techie. He'll probably just want to top and tail – go from one cue to the next, you know? So he understands the show and how the lighting plot fits and all that . . .'

Tamar gave a little nod and straightened her shoulders. Together they started down the passage towards the kitchen, but Beetle turned as he heard the squeak of the doors to the street behind him. He froze. Pasty White and Nick Spitz stood in the hallway.

'Go, go!'

Beetle shoved Tamar away down the passage. She glanced back, then ran. Greg and Beetle closed ranks as Pasty and Nick gave a hitch at their combats and eased into an insolent walk towards them.

Nick Spitz hawked and spat on the floor right at Greg's feet.

With a hiss of rage, Beetle leaped forward, but Greg slapped a hand on to his shoulder and heaved him back.

'Is that the best you can do, Nick *Spitz*?' he said.

'What did you call me?'

'You heard . . . Look at you, always at it, gobbed all down your jacket and all.'

Nick Spitz glanced down at his jacket but there wasn't a mark. He threw back his head to be met by Greg's finger tipping his nose. With a roar he pounced forward followed by Pasty White. Pasty grabbed at Greg, but Greg slid under his arm, elbowing him in the stomach, winding him. Nick pushed Beetle against the wall, fist raised, ready to hammer down into his face. From behind, Greg caught at his jacket and pulled it tight till the zip dug into his neck. Nick staggered back, ramming Greg into the wall behind as Beetle sprang forward, but Pasty White, recovered now, lashed out at him, knocking him sideways. Just as Beetle was beginning to wonder if they'd been wise to get into this, the doors burst open and three members of the steel band walked in.

'Got a little trouble here, friends?'

Rita was pushing five foot two in her bouncy trainers. She had bright blue eyes behind tiny gold-rimmed glasses, gold spiky hair, gold rings, lots of gold flashing round her shiny red and black shell suit and even a tiny gold tooth. She seemed to pluck Nick Spitz into the air and roll him over her back to dump him on one side. Another, a Vietnamese called Yip, whip-thin in green and white, separated Pasty White and Beetle, picking Pasty up bodily and depositing him near the door. The third, Buster, a stocky young black man in yellow with muscles like rope, picked him up and pinned him to the wall. At that moment, Ben hurried up the passage.

'I think it's time you gentlemen left,' he said.

Pasty and Nick looked daggers. They brushed themselves down.

'Don't worry. We don't want to stay in your poncey little cabaret, *guv*.'

They looked the three musicians up and down in disgust.

'We don't like the company you keep.'

The musicians gave a hoot of laughter.

'Fine,' said Rita, brushing off her hands. 'Leave when you like and don't come back until you change your attitude. Everyone's welcome here, even you, if you behave. If not . . .'

With a smirk of derision the two lads pushed through the doors.

Ben turned to Greg and Beetle.

'That goes for you two as well. No fighting in The Hall. You know the rules.'

They nodded, crestfallen.

'It wasn't us,' said Beetle. 'We didn't start it.'

'I know,' said Ben, 'but . . .'

'You have problems,' Rita said to Ben, 'we'll see to it, no sweat. We know their kind – and *we* don't like the company *they* keep.'

She jerked her head towards the door and her tiny gold-rimmed glasses flickered.

'Remember,' she said, 'we're not just a bunch of pretty tunes.'

Ben laughed.

'Too right. I don't think we'll have any trouble with you lot around,' he said. 'Come on, you two, let's get on with things.'

Greg would clearly have liked to have discussed the niceties of martial arts with the three musicians, but Ben ushered him down the passage in front of him. Beetle followed slowly as Rita gave his shoulder a squeeze, making him wince.

No, he thought, no trouble while you're around, but what about when you're not?

For he had seen the knife in Nick Spitz's back pocket as he banged out through the doors.

Chapter 9

Inside the auditorium, the working lights were on, the curtain was open, revealing an empty stage, and the pianist was running his hands up and down the keys in an aimless kind of way. Nothing much seemed to be happening at all, like many a technical rehearsal before. Greg had disappeared to the dressing-rooms and Beetle slumped on to a bench. He was worried about Pasty White and Nick Spitz now that war seemed to be openly declared between them. Oh yes, he and Greg could take them on, no sweat, but that had been a close thing, and suppose they weren't always together. And the knife – was that for show or would Nick Spitz use it?

He put his feet up on the bench in front, his shoulders hunched up round his ears.

'Ahem.'

Hastily, Beetle sat up. It can't have been Old Mitch, he wouldn't have coughed, he would have simply come and shoved his feet off the bench. The sound seemed to have come from above. For one wonderful moment, Beetle thought it might be Zak, but when he looked up, Mr Daniels was leaning with both arms outstretched on the balcony rail, looking down at him.

'Bums on seats, my boy, not feet.'

He couldn't have been joking, could he? Beetle half-smiled.

'Sorry,' he said, in case he was serious, and moved his feet.

Mr Daniels gave a little nod.

'I think you'll find there's a cable loose on the floor up at the far end there. Not safe. Needs some new gaffer tape.'

Beetle scrambled to his feet, side-stepped along the row of benches and looked along the line of cables taped down to the floor. Sure enough, up near the stage, the old gaffer tape had become scuffed up, leaving the cable exposed. Beetle looked up.

'I'll go and get the—'

But Mr Daniels had vanished and Beetle could hear him moving about up above. With a little leap of pleasure inside him, Beetle went to the workroom, sorted out some tape, came back and fastened down the cable that Zak and he had put down together. He paused for a moment. 'Zak and he' – they had always made very sure that everything was secure. When they taped down cables, they almost never came up. He looked at the tape he had just taken up. The break was very clean, as if it had been cut. Surely Mr Daniels hadn't . . . ?

'A good job you've made there, my boy. Did you do all those others too?'

'Me and Zak. I'll go and put the tape away.'

'Thanks. Oh and while you're there, the Number 36 gel in the fresnel up here is burning through. Could you cut another and bring it up?'

'Sure – but – up there?'

'Just bring it to the balcony door and I'll collect it.'

Beetle hurried back to the workroom and spent a satisfying ten minutes sorting out gels, cutting beautiful straight lines with the Stanley knife, finding a frame and fitting the gel into it. Then he scampered through the auditorium, up the front stairs, opened the balcony door and stuck his head in.

'There you go,' he said, holding out the gel frame.

Mr Daniels creaked up the steps towards him. He took long enough for Beetle to have a quick look round the balcony. Nothing had changed. The great chandeliers still cast shadows from the working lights, stage lamps still hung like sentinels over the vast space, and dust, dust everywhere. Mr Daniels wheezed.

'All this dust. Not too good for my chest,' he said, taking the gel and examining it closely. 'That's eh, that's very good, my boy.'

' 'S OK,' said Beetle, pleased. 'Zak showed me how. I like doing all that stuff. Anything else you want doing?'

From the lighting desk below them on the balcony, he heard the tinny sound of Ben's voice over the mike of the head-set hanging on the lamp bracket.

'Not right now, thanks,' said Mr Daniels. 'That'll be Mr Starkey ready to start. Off you go.'

'I'm always around if you need me.'

'So I see,' said Mr Daniels, and Beetle could have sworn there was the vestige of a twinkle in those stony eyes. He galloped downstairs, giving the door on the landing a hefty kick for old times' sake.

He settled into the auditorium to watch. How would Mr Daniels cope with the plot of a show he had never seen before? Was he really as good as Kiley's gran had said? The working lights were out now, the curtain down and the house lights on. The pianist stopped tinkling about and waited, examining his nails over his glasses. Then the house lights dimmed and he sprang to life, flexing his fingers and taking a quick look at the programme order on the music stand in front of him. Tum ta-ta, ta-ta-ta taaaah! He crashed out a fanfare and, with a flourish, Greg emerged through the curtains covering the pass door. He sprang on to his little platform into the pool of light that opened like a flower to meet him. Perfect timing. Beetle relaxed in the darkness of the auditorium and surreptitiously slid his feet back on to the bench in front. Instantly, they were knocked off again by Old Mitch, as he and Brian slipped into the row behind.

'Naughty, naughteeee,' said Brian, splashily.

Beetle grinned and wiped the back of his neck with his sleeve. Suddenly, it felt like he belonged in The Hall again.

The show began. Most people wanted to do some bits of their act, 'just to make sure'. Only the Wilson Brothers really 'topped and tailed', since they felt it was 'pretty good the way it was'.

Pretty terrible, more like, thought Beetle, but as he watched the show progress, he became more and more impressed as, up above, Mr Daniels slid faultlessly from cue to cue. Jamey's Indian clubs swooped and glittered, Rita and the steel band dazzled, the dancing-class frills sparkled like icing sugar. 'Cross-fades as smooth as a baby's bottom,' Beetle heard Old Mitch whisper to Brian, and Brian cackled back quietly.

A sudden draught shivered through the auditorium as the pass door opened and some of the dancing-class kids tiptoed in with tiny clicks of their tap shoes. Kiley and her mum sat across the aisle from Beetle, which gave Kiley the chance to wiggle a long pink tongue at him as she passed. He pointedly ignored her, turning his attention to Greg, who was getting ready for his big introduction for Tamar.

Beetle glanced at the door. There still seemed to be a cold draught from somewhere. He hadn't heard Old Mitch and Brian leave, but the bench behind was empty now. Perhaps the main auditorium doors at the back were open – but no, everything was still and dark, except for some people in the back rows. Some of them seemed to be eating. Old Mitch would go wild if he caught them. One even looked as if he had a pint of beer. Perhaps they'd strayed in from the pub across the road, friends of Mr Daniels maybe, come to see how he was doing. Ben wouldn't be too pleased either.

Beetle turned back to the stage.

'Dee-licious, de-ee-lightful, dee-ee-lectable . . .'

Funny, Greg's voice seemed to have dropped an

octave or two – and surely the fanfare was coming from a trumpet, cracked and a bit out of tune, but definitely brassy, nothing like a piano.

The auditorium went dark and a gust of wind swirled past Beetle, setting his skin on edge, as if a goose had walked over his grave. Shadows of people seemed to surround him now, faceless and unreal. He almost reached out to touch the man nearest him just to make sure there was someone there, but drew back, suddenly afraid that his hand might meet with nothing, nothing at all – but that was stupid. He sat on his hands.

The curtain went up and there was Tamar, picked out in her gold light. He looked round. Where had all those people gone? The auditorium was deserted, and yet there was a whispering and rustling coming from somewhere, like a big audience getting ready for a favourite act. The sounds died away to silence as Tamar started to sing.

But who was with her? Behind Tamar, on the edge of the pool of light, stood a woman in a long purple dress. For a moment there was an unnatural silence. The figures seemed to blur and merge, now Tamar in the light, now the woman. Then their voices burst out, now one louder, now the other, like a radio ebbing and flowing in and out of tune, first Tamar's lone voice and then the woman's, singing a song Beetle didn't recognize. She was backed by a band, brassy and blaring. But where was it? The music came and went, louder and louder, in a nightmare of sound.

Beetle wanted to move, to shut his eyes, to get away. But he couldn't. Waves of cold washed over him, and a trickle of icy sweat ran down between his shoulder blades. He put his hands over his ears, but still he could see the two singers fading and looming in and out of the light on the stage, their mouths opening and shutting as they sang on and on, sounds he could not bear to hear.

Then she disappeared. The woman in the long dress vanished into the darkness at the back of the stage, and Tamar stood alone, singing as if nothing had happened. Hardly daring to listen, Beetle took his hands from his ears. But there was just Tamar, her voice now low like a bell, now high, echoing round and round the auditorium like the wind round a steeple.

And Beetle looked up.

The little girl in white stood on the balcony, leaning through the railing, her arms reaching out, towards Tamar, her mouth stretched wide as if trying to call out – but no sound came. A blue light seemed to flicker round her. Beetle shifted and she turned. Her huge eyes looked straight down, straight into his. She seemed to take a breath to speak but her voice could only come in drifts, lost in Tamar's song.

'B . . . b . . . bo-o-y . . . Ta-a . . . t-a-a-ake . . .'

Beetle jumped to his feet and flung an arm up towards her.

'Look! Look! She's—'

But she wasn't. She was gone.

Far above, Beetle heard a door slam. What had she been trying to say? And was she saying it to him? He turned to run, to look for her, to tell someone, to do something, anything – but suddenly he felt Old Mitch's hand on his shoulder.

'Sit down, lad.'

'But didn't you see—?'

'No, I didn't. There was nothing to see. You didn't see anything.'

'I did, I did. She was there.'

'Ssssh. You'll have Ben out here in a minute. Sit down.'

Beetle sat down. Stiffly and painfully, Old Mitch clambered over the bench to sit beside him. Tamar had finished and the Senior Citizens Choir was assembling behind the curtain.

'That's better.'

Old Mitch spoke in a whisper and turned to quieten Brian who was trying to move forward with him.

'Stay there, Brian, I'm not far away, look.'

Brian mumbled but kept still.

'I saw that girl,' said Beetle, keeping his voice down with an effort.

'Shush, will you?'

'I – saw – that – girl.'

'There was nothing, lad. I've been here all the time and I'd have seen—'

'You weren't here. You left—'

'No, Beetle, we've been here right through the show. Both of us. Right behind you.'

Beetle looked at him. Old Mitch met his eyes. He was telling the truth.

'And you didn't see . . .?'

'No, lad, nothing. There was nothing to see. You imagined it.'

Beetle grew angry.

'I didn't. I didn't.'

'Shut up now, lad, this isn't the moment. Later. We'll talk about it later.'

Seething with fury, Beetle sat still, picking at the bubbles of paint on the bench with one finger, his head bent, ignoring the stage. For once, Old Mitch did nothing to stop him. He put an arm across his shoulder, but Beetle shrugged it away. Hardly able to contain himself, he sat through *Daisy, Daisy* and the rest. It seemed to take for ever, but at last the curtain fell. The house lights went up.

'Fancy making all that noise, Beetle. You were terrible.'

Kiley's voice broke into his thoughts like squeaky chalk on a blackboard. Had she been there all the time too? He glared at her, but her mother pulled her to her feet.

'No one'll ever call *you* a little trouper, Beetle, you don't know how to behave when a show's on, you don't.'

'Shut – up – Kiley.'

Beetle was stiff with rage. Again, Old Mitch's hand went to his shoulder. Kiley's mother began to lead Kiley away, when Mr Daniels came into the auditorium through the back doors.

'Fred!' said Old Mitch. 'You old devil. You haven't missed a trick, have you?'

'Trick,' said Brian, 'missed trick.'

Mr Daniels managed to look almost pleased. He pushed a gentle fist against Brian's cheek.

'Quite like old times,' he said.

'Did you see her?' Beetle couldn't help himself.

He wanted to say how brilliant Mr Daniels had been too, but he had to settle this once and for all first . . .

'See who? I saw a great deal going on from up there, young man.'

'No, no. I don't mean on the stage, I mean up there, with you, on the balcony.'

'On the balcony?'

In vain, Old Mitch frowned at Beetle, trying to shut him up.

'The little girl. The little girl who leans over . . . and then, and then . . . goes through the door. The door bangs and she's gone.'

'I certainly did not. If I had, I'd have stopped the show. It's dangerous up there.'

'But, but . . . someone else must have seen her. She was *there*!'

'Reckon you're seeing things,' said Mr Daniels. Suddenly, he caught his breath and began to cough. He coughed and coughed, getting red in the face.

'It's – it's – this – du—'

He couldn't finish the sentence. He slumped on to the bench, unable to stop coughing. Old Mitch began to pat and rub his back, his face screwed up with anxiety.

'Brian, go and get a glass of water, quick.'

Brian lumbered away, muttering, 'Quick, quick.'

'It's the dust. Always been his trouble. It brings on his asthma if he isn't careful. It's why he had to retire early.'

'I'll – be – be . . .'

But what Mr Daniels would be, Beetle didn't stay to find out. People were beginning to gather round the figure fighting for breath on the bench. He would be taken care of. Beetle was forgotten. With a last, lingering look up at the dark, empty balcony, he went backstage to find Greg.

Chapter 10

'I did see her, I did.'

'OK, man. Cool it. Yelling at me isn't going to—'

'Nobody believes me. They think I'm a nutter, or something.'

'Look, I believe you. Let's get out of here, then we can talk.'

Carefully, so carefully that Beetle was driven almost mad with impatience, Greg tidied his make-up desk, tweaked a couple of imaginary hairs from his costume, put it on a hanger and hung it up on the rail at the end of the dressing-room. It glittered in the bright lights round the mirrors on each dressing-table. Beetle caught sight of his own reflection. He saw a pale face with angry red spots on each cheek and eyes that looked kind of funny, kind of sunk back in his head. He dragged the heels of his hands over them and swung away quickly to shut out the sight of himself. Greg turned out all the lights and they went out past the auditorium where a few voices were still buzzing away anxiously, but at least Mr Daniels seemed to have stopped coughing.

'I'm telling you—'

'Shut up, a minute, will you?'

Greg dragged Beetle into a doorway and looked out, up and down the street.

'No sign of them,' he said. 'Anyway, Tamar went home with her mum ages ago. But you never know . . .'

'Never mind those two gits,' said Beetle. 'This is serious. Why won't anyone believe me – about the kid up there?'

'Dunno. Maybe it's because – because . . .'

'You think I'm making it up, too, don't you?'

'No, no I don't, not now, but—'

'Forget it! I'm out of here . . .'

Beetle pushed past him. Greg caught his arm, dragged him back into the doorway, shoved him against the wall and stared at him, eyeball to eyeball.

'Look, this isn't the time or the place. Those two may be anywhere. Not that I'm scared or anything, but I'd like to do the show with all my teeth, man.'

'We can handle them,' said Beetle, deliberately shutting the memory of the knife from his mind. He could only worry about one thing at a time.

'Yeah. Well, maybe. It was pretty close back there, before Rita and—'

'Do *you* think I'm a nutter?'

' 'Course not. No way. It's just that – can't we talk about it tomorrow? My mum'll be waiting to go to work and she likes to see me before she—'

'Aren't you the lucky one.'

It wasn't a question. Beetle was hunched up into his shoulders, but suddenly gave himself a little shake, threw Greg a quick, fierce glance and let out a breath. Greg dropped his eyes and leant against the opposite wall of the doorway, bumping against it with his back, to and fro, to and fro.

'Yeah. Well . . .'

Bundles of greasy papers, crisp packets and empty cans shifted round Beetle's ankles and he kicked them away, shoving his hands deep into his pockets. He drove his heel hard into a burger box. It burst with a bang that made Greg jump. A half-eaten meal spilled on to the grimy grey tiles; soggy onions, blackened meat and dead chips lay everywhere. Beetle looked around at them.

' 'S about how I feel,' he said. He kicked the box into the gutter and slouched out of the doorway after it. Chips and onions scattered over the pavement.

Greg followed, trying to step through the mess, but squashing it and slipping and sliding about.

'All I'm saying is—' he said.

'All you're saying is, you don't believe me, I'm seeing things, and I'm some kind of nutter. Right?'

Beetle turned to face him.

'Right?'

Greg gave his head a vigorous rub with both hands, then looked up.

'You wanna know what I think? I'll tell you. I think you did see something. I think Old Mitch knows you saw something, and maybe Kiley's gran does too, but no one wants to talk about it, because they don't like it and they don't want the kids scared. But whatever it is – it's not as important as those two and Tamar. And I don't want to talk about any of it now. I want to go home, see my— have a pizza and forget about it.'

'Great.'

'Look. It'll be—'

'Don't tell me. Better in the morning. You piss me off sometimes, Greg, honest.'

Beetle turned tail and stumped off, and for once, Greg didn't follow him. He watched him go. Somehow he seemed to look small under the lights, a tight knot of anger waiting to explode. Just then, the doors of The Hall opened and Ben Starkey hurried out. He looked up and down the street anxiously, craning his neck to listen for something.

'Where the hell are they?'

'Who?'

Greg immediately thought of Pasty White and Nick Spitz.

'They're taking their time. We rang ages ago.'

'Who?'

'The ambulance of course. They must know where we are. Everyone knows The Hall.'

'What for? What's the matter?'

Had those two got back inside The Hall? Had there been a fight? Who was hurt? But Ben hurried back inside without answering, too worried to speak. He hardly seemed to have registered Greg was there.

Greg followed him. There was still a buzz of voices from inside the auditorium. Brian was shuffling up the passage with a glass of water, trying to hurry.

'What's the trouble?' said Greg.

'Trouble,' said Brian. 'Bad, bad, bad.'

He shook his head, spilling some water down his jumper, and muttered his way past into the auditorium. Greg peered in. No sign of anyone looking as if they'd been causing trouble, just a knot of people huddled round a figure propped up against a bench with Old Mitch kneeling beside him. Next to Old Mitch, Ben had taken the glass of water and was bending forwards, shielding the slumped shape from Greg's view.

Outside, further up the street, Beetle didn't notice the ambulance slide past him and nose to a halt outside The Hall. The paramedics in their hospital greens gathered up their rubber gloves and went inside as Greg came out. There seemed to be enough people fussing round whoever it was. There was no sign of Pasty White or Nick Spitz or any other kind of trouble and his mum and his pizza were waiting.

Across the market, Beetle heard the clang of the ambulance in the distance but it was a common enough noise round there, specially at night. Besides, he was too occupied with other things to bother about it. Greg was right, he supposed, the big problem was Nick Spitz and Pasty and keeping Tamar safe. He turned into an alley with a high brick wall running down one side and on the other, iron railings holding back spiky bushes full of thorns. At the far end an ancient metal bollard gleamed in the street light. It seemed to stand sentinel. The grey metal shone the colour of the great eyes of the little girl on the balcony. For a moment, it was as if she were standing there, waiting for him, a silent, solitary figure, waiting . . . almost warning him . . .

He put both hands up to his head and rubbed them up and down hard, shaking himself free of her. He galloped down the alley and looked both ways before turning left. Away to the right, two figures were sauntering up the street. They could have been Nick and Pasty but he wasn't sure. Whoever they were, they were going away from him and hadn't seen him. He waited in the shelter of the alley until they had turned a corner then ran, dodging the litter, the pot-holes and the broken paving stones, till he reached the tower block and the long, lonely climb up to his flat.

Six floors up, he paused on the landing outside Kiley's gran's front door, but there was no light underneath and suddenly, he was too tired to face the effort of persuading her to open up for him, and anyway, she would tell him nothing, he was sure. He'd try in the morning. On he went, slower and slower. There was no light under his door either. He let himself in and went to the kitchen. There was nothing in the tiny fridge but a wedge of dry old cheese, a half bottle of milk with lumps in it and a couple of cans of beer. He took a handful of dry cereal from an open packet on the table and fumbled his way to his small, stuffy bedroom without putting on the light. He shoved some of the cereal into his mouth, but it was dry and tasteless and he tongued it away in disgust. For a moment he sat with his elbows on his knees, crunching the rest in his fist. He dropped his head. Sure he could take care of himself. No sweat. Slowly, kicking off his shoes and dropping his clothes around him on the floor, he crawled into the bed that was as he had left it that morning. He fell asleep with cornflakes all over the crumpled grey sheet beneath him.

Chapter 11

A crack of greenish light through a hole in the curtain woke Beetle from a troubled sleep full of shadowy dreams of eyes following him, eerie voices singing, strangely mixed up with Nick Spitz and Pasty White trying to strangle him with a white dress. He woke to find himself sweating, his arms tangled in the sheet, his thin pillow half over his face. He pushed it off and lay for a moment breathing heavily, wondering why his stomach felt empty but heavy all at the same time. Then he remembered. Well, hunger would have to wait and anyway, the fridge would still be empty. He would have to deal with the heavy feeling that went with having no one to believe him about the kid on the balcony. He couldn't decide who to tackle first, Kiley's gran, or Old Mitch. Old Mitch knew more he was sure, but it would be harder to get him to talk. Kiley's gran, well, was Kiley's gran and it would depend on her mood and whether Kiley was around or not. He decided to play it by ear. He turned over, steamrollering the cornflakes, and leapt out of bed.

'Ugh!'

Brushing cereal dust from as many places as he could reach, he pulled on his clothes, hitched on his long key chain, peered in at his mum – or what he could see of her under the old blankets piled on her bed – and went out, slamming the door behind him. He half ran down the stairs, half slid down the metal rail. It caught on his jeans, almost ripping the pocket.

He set off towards Greg's. Greg's nan had been known to provide breakfast if Beetle looked hungry enough, but he suddenly remembered Greg the night before – saying he believed him about seeing that kid but just wanting to go home like a wimp and not wanting to do anything about it. Times like this you needed people you could depend on, best mate or no. Greg could come looking for him. No way would he go looking for Greg.

In the market, Kiley's gran was busy setting out the stall. Without a word, Beetle started to give her a hand, shifting the display about a bit, making everything look tempting, irresistible.

'You're really good at this, young Beetle. Give you a job any time.'

'OK,' said Beetle, 'you're on.'

He picked up a tureen with a lid and went to put it in pride of place in the centre of the stall, but his hand slipped and the lid slid forwards. Kiley's gran just got a hand to it as it fell.

'Ooops. That was a lucky one.'

'Sorry,' said Beetle. 'I . . .' – and he sat down on the pavement and dropped his head on to his arms, suddenly heavy with dejection.

Kiley's gran put down the lid. She crouched down beside him, putting an arm round his shoulders.

'Here, you're shaking like a leaf, love. What's the matter?'

'Nothing. I'm all right. Bit cold, that's all.'

'Cold? On a morning like this?'

She took his hand and gave it a rub.

'You are too. Here, have you had any breakfast?'

He shook his head, not looking up.

'Not hungry.'

'And last night? Supper?'

He shrugged.

'Watch the stall a minute.'

Kiley's gran hurried away into the snack bar across the road and a few moments later returned, with a large take-away cup of hot chocolate and a fried egg sandwich that draped itself over the ends of its paper plate and oozed melted marge.

'Here, get that inside you. I don't know . . . Some people shouldn't have k—'

She glanced at him but something in the look in his eyes made her stop short.

'Come on, love, eat it up. You'll feel better then.'

Still sitting on the edge of the pavement, Beetle wolfed down the sandwich and licked his fingers.

'Good?'

'I'll say. Thanks. Thanks a lot.'

He took up the chocolate and blew on it, folding his hands round it, gathering warmth. He looked up at Kiley's gran.

'There's something I—'

But a customer interrupted him and Kiley's gran went round the front of the stall to look at plates and talk prices. Beetle took a sip of the chocolate but it was hot and he put it down beside him. Suddenly, the cup flew into the air, spilling the drink and splattering his jeans with brown liquid that soaked through, burning his skin.

'Oh dear, oh dear, oh dear, I *am* sorry. Clumsy, clumsy. I wonder how that happened?'

Beetle didn't have to look up. He turned and lunged for the ankle in the high-tops but Pasty White was quicker on his feet than his size suggested he might be, and he dodged away, laughing all over his pasty face, his teeth yellow and foul in the sunlight.

'Sod off,' said Beetle, but without bothering to get up and give chase.

'Naughty, naughty,' said Pasty. 'What language. I dunno.'

He ran backwards away from the stall, laughing even more.

'Don't worry, I'll get you later,' said Beetle, but still without moving. He watched fascinated as Pasty, still smirking, backed further and further across the road towards the opposite stall, covered in toys and radios. With a crash, Pasty backed right into it, knocking dolls and model cars, colouring books and crayons, games and boxes of bricks all over the street. The stall-holder gave a yell and grabbed Pasty by the arm.

'Oi, you. Look where you're going. If there's anything bust, you'll pay for it. Now pick 'em up, you hear me? You pick 'em all up, every last one.'

'It wasn't my fault, it was him – over there.'

Pasty jabbed a stubby finger towards Beetle, who, trying to look unperturbed, sat giggling behind his hand.

'Oh no it wasn't. And I saw you kick his cup over.

You just get on with it or I'll call Old Bill.'

Pasty shrugged the man off roughly and started to gather the things up and dump them in a heap on the stall.

'No you don't. You put them back properly. I'm watching you.'

The stall-holder was a big man. You could tell just by looking at him that he did serious weight-training. Killing him with a look, Pasty picked everything up and left the stall more or less tidy, before turning to give Beetle a vicious two fingers and hurrying off. Beetle just nodded with a grin, and waved two indolent fingers back again.

I will. I'll get you later, he thought to himself. Pasty was nothing on his own. Nick was a different matter, but Pasty . . . huh. Still, Pasty would be really angry right now. He was doubtless off to find Nick for a good moan. Better keep his eyes open.

Kiley's gran returned and sat on her upturned crate beside him.

'Oh . . . Beetle! You've spilt your chocolate. And look, it's all over your jeans. Here!'

She began to wipe him with her duster. Gently, Beetle stopped her. His leg was a bit tender and anyway, he didn't want a fuss.

'You won't get it off with that. Don't worry, I'll

take 'em to the laundrette some time. It's not much – I'd nearly finished it,' he said, with his fingers crossed behind his back. No way would he let her buy him a second cup and she might try. She had that look in her eye.

'There's something . . . something I want to ask you,' he said.

'What's that, love?'

'It's about The Hall . . . about the – the ghost . . .'

Kiley's gran swivelled away from him on her crate, looking annoyed.

'Now then, Beetle. I've told you . . . it's all eye-wash. Just stories. Everyone loves a ghost story, specially about an old place like that with all those nooks and crannies . . .'

'Honest? But – but I keep seeing this kid, this little girl. Up on the balcony, she is, looking over, and when I go towards her, she isn't there. And everything goes kind of weird. I thought it was one of Kiley's mates at first, so then they locked the door, but there she was again. Last night . . .'

He gabbled on, hardly drawing breath. He reached out and tugged her round to face him. She pulled his hand away.

'Beetle, don't do that. You're hurting me. I'm telling you there isn't a ghost . . .'

'It's because you don't want that Kiley scared, isn't it? Isn't it?'

'It's not just Kiley, it's all those little ones. They love their dancing class, and they wouldn't go near the place if they knew . . . I mean if they thought . . . it was haunted.'

'Knew. You said knew. There is one. There *is* a ghost. I knew it. I knew it.'

A terrible wail set in behind him. He looked round.

'Gra-a-a-n, Gra-a-a-n, you said there wasn't one. You promised. You said there wasn't a ghost. And now there is . . .'

'Beetle, I could kill you,' said Kiley's gran. 'Now look what you've done.'

She stood up, took Kiley's hand, drew her towards the crate and sat her on her lap, giving her little consoling pats, turning her ringlet bunches over her fingers, murmuring to her.

'No, love, it isn't true. Don't you worry, now.'

'But he said—'

'Never mind him. It's only boys' stuff . . . You know, silly stories.'

'I don't want to go to The Hall ever again, not ever.'

'But you've got the show. It's the last rehearsal tonight and then tomorrow . . .'

'I'm not going! I'm not going! And I'm going to tell all my friends too!'

Kiley's voice reached a piercing shriek that turned heads the length of the market. Beetle stood up with a sigh. Trust Kiley. What a moment to choose to turn up behind them, just as he was getting somewhere.

'Sorry,' he said in a low voice, 'and thanks for the – the sandwich and all.'

But Kiley's gran was busy trying to quieten Kiley, whose fingers were bunching up her pink mini-skirt so tightly everyone could see the top of her lacy tights. As fast as her Gran smoothed her down, Kiley clutched another bit of skirt and her round pink tummy peeped out and great sobs issued from her round pink mouth. Beetle edged away.

'Oh there you are,' said a voice behind him. 'Thank goodness I've found you.'

Beetle turned, puzzled.

'Me?'

'Yes, you.'

Ben Starkey, looking hot and anxious, stood behind him.

'Listen, come back to The Hall with me, will you?'

'I haven't done anything,' said Beetle, frantically searching his mind and hoping it was true.

'I know, I know,' said Ben, pushing him in front

of him and setting off for The Hall at a trot. Inside, he leant against the door and wiped his forehead with the back of his hand.

'Pphhh . . . Thank goodness I've found you. I even went up to that flat of yours – all the way up those stairs. Why aren't you on the phone, young Beetle? Anyway, I've got you now.'

'If it's about the kid on the balcony . . .'

'What? No. Don't be stupid. That's got nothing to do with anything. Just shut up about it. This is serious.'

He lowered himself on to the bottom stair and patted it for Beetle to sit beside him.

'It's the show,' he said.

'What about it?'

'Well . . . I'm going to break the rules, Beetle. I've no alternative. I can't find anyone else at this short notice. Not for tonight, anyway. Zak just might be able to get back for the show itself tomorrow but certainly not for tonight – and we must do a proper dress . . . there's been enough upsets and changes as it is.'

'But what about Mr Daniels? He was brilliant.'

'He's in hospital. Didn't you see the ambulance last night? The dust up there brought on an asthma attack, and with his size, they're afraid of his heart.'

Beetle was aghast. Just as he was getting to like – well, if not like, to think he wasn't too bad. And he *was* brilliant. It had been a joy to watch him glide through the lighting plot as if he'd been doing it for ever. And he might have taught him a thing or two, like Kiley's gran had said.

'He'll be all right, won't he?'

'Sure. But not to come for tonight. I doubt he'll ever be able to come back to work at The Hall.'

'So . . .'

'So it'll have to be you, Beetle.'

'Me? But—'

'I know. You aren't supposed to be up there. The insurance would have a fit and I know it's a risk, but . . . there's no other way round it. But you must promise, Beetle, promise . . . You sit at the desk and you don't leave it. You understand me? I don't care if – if – Napoleon and his army turn up up there, you – do – not – move.'

'Promise.'

Beetle swallowed hard, then he looked at Ben.

'You know I won't. No matter what happens. I won't leave the desk.'

'And I won't leave the corner, not for anything, so you'll be able to contact me every second. I'll ask Miss James to stay with the dancing-class kids and

I'll see if Jamey will hang around when he's not on stage to run messages and look after emergencies. Can you do it, Beetle?'

'Do it? The show? Of course I can.'

'We'd better go up and run through the plot a couple of times and make sure everything up there is OK.'

Beetle jumped up.

'OK. Let's go.'

Ben blew out his cheeks again.

'I'm getting too old for all this,' he said with a grin, heaving himself up. 'It'll be me in hospital next if this goes on. Come on then. And when we've done this, I'll buy you a sandwich if you behave yourself.'

But Beetle hadn't heard. He was way ahead, already half-way up the stairs, and the stairwell echoed to the sound of a passing kick at the door on the landing.

Chapter 12

Time flew by. Beetle and Ben ran through the plot six
or seven times, checking here, tightening up cues
there. They re-covered cables, changed a couple
of gels and tested the intercom system over and
over. Neither of them mentioned the little girl on the
balcony, but while Beetle was sweeping the stage, he
heard Ben go up the backstage stairs and check that
the door at the top was locked.

So Ben thought she was real, did he? Well, Beetle
thought otherwise. But she was a strange kind of
ghost, more scared than scary. From down here she
was, anyway. He glanced up at the balcony. Why did
she come? What had she been trying to say?

Ben came clattering down the stairs and Beetle
hurriedly got on with the sweeping. At half-past four,
after a quick fish and chips up the market with Ben,
Beetle suddenly remembered Tamar. Would she be
coming on her own, or would her mum be coming

to see her in the final dress rehearsal? Would Greg go and fetch her? Someone must.

Beetle zigzagged his way through the streets towards Ransome House and the flat over the little shop with the graffiti. He glanced at the TV shop with its flickering screens, but didn't stop. He turned the corner to wait in a doorway, impatiently jigging up and down from foot to foot. After a moment, Tamar came out with her mother. They seemed to be arguing. Her mother locked the door and marched up the road holding on tightly to Tamar's arm. Suddenly, Tamar's mother dragged her to a halt. They leant towards each other, both talking at once, their voices hushed but urgent. One of Tamar's hands jerked up and down vehemently, emphasising a point. At last, reluctantly, her mother turned back the way they had come. She looked distressed. Tamar called after her:

'I am all right, Mother. Please. Just come later to see the rehearsal, you don't need to come now. I am all right.'

Her mother didn't answer, so Tamar shouted out in Kurdish, seeming to repeat what she had said, but her mother just shook her head, let herself in through their door and slammed it behind her. Tamar sighed and looked worried. She started on towards The

Hall, then turned back, then turned again as if trying to make up her mind what to do. Then she shrugged, squared her shoulders and set off with her head held high under her veil. At that moment, Greg appeared at the other end of the street. He waved at her.

'Hi, Tamar! You coming to rehearsal?'

'Yes. It's all right, Greg. My mother isn't coming till later, but I am fine on my own.'

'No sweat. I'm going that way – unless you don't want company.'

Tamar relaxed and laughed.

'Of course I would like company. Let's go together. Listen, you know the bit of the show when I . . .'

She hurried to catch up with Greg and Beetle heard no more as they disappeared round the corner. Still not in the mood to talk to Greg yet, he followed. He was about to turn right after them, when something made him glance up to his left. In a flash he slid into a doorway. Pasty White and Nick Spitz were sauntering down the road. They spotted Tamar and Greg ahead and started to gather speed.

The two of them together – and Tamar and Greg were still some way from The Hall.

Beetle dodged out in front of them and danced about on the pavement, gesturing, 'come on, come on' with both hands. They hesitated, not certain whether to go for him or follow Tamar.

'What's the matter – running scared?' said Beetle, still dancing away from them, backwards.

'Scared of you, you . . .' said Nick on a hissed breath. 'Try me,' and he launched himself forward.

But Beetle was too fast. He was across the road, up the alley, vaulting the bollard on the way. The two boys followed him, but stopped at the entrance. Beetle turned at the far end and gestured for them to 'come on', again. They took a step or two forwards and Pasty's jacket caught on a branch of one of the spiky bushes. He wrenched himself free, tearing his sleeve and cannoning into the high wall. He swore violently and turned to Nick. They muttered to each other for a moment, then Nick Spitz spat copiously and yelled:

'Oi, you! We'll get you later, no sweat. Can't be arsed with you now.'

'Yeah, yeah,' said Beetle, and came down the alley to watch them strolling down the street Clearly, they no longer intended to catch up with Greg and Tamar, but, bristly heads together, were immersed in their own nasty little world. Nick Spitz patted his back pocket and laughed.

Beetle cut back up through the alley and legged it to The Hall just in time to see Greg and Tamar going through the front doors, unaware of what had been happening behind them.

Beetle slipped into the newsagent's for a Mars bar and a Coke bought with money Ben had given him. As he came out, he looked back along the market. Nick Spitz and Pasty White stood at the fruit stall. They seemed to be bargaining with Mr Ginley and Pasty was holding a bulging plastic bag. Nick stooped down, picked up an apple lying in the street and stuffed it into the bag. Beetle's face creased up in puzzlement – what were they doing buying fruit? And even though they lived on fags and chips and worse as far as he knew, surely even they hadn't descended to picking stuff up from the pavement and eating it? He shook his head and went into The Hall.

He slipped into the Gents just inside the door, and began to focus on the rehearsal ahead. Tamar was safely here and Nick and Pasty were unlikely to go right into the theatre part of The Hall; there were too many people about. And anyway they'd see Rita and the steel band arriving. That would keep them away.

As he washed his hands, the cool water running over his fingers suddenly turned icy cold. He shivered and glanced up into the old cracked mirror above the basin. Someone was looking over his shoulder, someone small, with great eyes, dressed all in white. She held her hands either side of her head, staring as though in terror. She shook her head slowly and opened her mouth to speak.

He whipped round. There was no one, no one at all. Hurriedly, he wiped his hands on his jeans, looked into each cubicle and then out into the corridor. She wasn't there. But she had been, she had been, he was sure. She must have been standing in mid-air to see over his shoulder like that. If he hadn't turned round quickly like that, what would she have said? For a moment or two he waited, in case she came back, then slowly, trying to keep calm, told himself that everyone would say it must have been his imagination again – yet again . . . but it wasn't, it couldn't be. It had happened too often now to be just in his head. Giving himself a shake, he walked down the corridor towards the auditorium. He must keep it together; there was a show to do. This girl . . . this ghost . . . whatever she was, mustn't get in the way this time.

He opened the door. There was pandemonium. Beetle could hear raised voices, shrill and protesting, coming from the room behind the kitchen. There seemed to be dozens of kids in there, yelling their heads off, and Ben and Miss James over the top of them, trying to calm them down. Behind him, the doors swung open.

'I won't, I won't go in.'

'Don't be silly, love. It's all right, there's nothing to be afraid of.'

'Oh yes there is . . . there's a ghost, there is . . .'

Kiley. Kiley in her spangled tap-dance costume and enormous shiny bows on her bunches, her fat little knees stiff in protest as her mother alternately tugged and propelled her into The Hall. Finally, her mother gave up and stopped in the passage. She glared at Beetle as she caught sight of him.

'I suppose you're well pleased . . .'

'Me?' said Beetle. 'I never—'

'Oh yes you did, you said there was a ghost. You said my gran said . . . Well, I'm not going in, so there, fish face. The show'll be ruined and it's all your fault.'

'See?'

Kiley's mother looked at him with the kind of angry but smug expression that said she was quite happy to blame him for everything.

Ben emerged from the fracas.

'For crying out loud, Beetle, what did you want to go and do that for?'

'I didn't do anything . . . I was just asking Kiley's gran about – you know – that kid up there and *she*' –

he jerked his head at Kiley – '*she* took it as gospel.'

'Well, she would, wouldn't she?' said Ben with a sigh. The noise in the back room seemed to have diminished a little.

'Come on, Kiley, there's nothing to be frightened of. No ghosts. No spooks. Nothing. Are there, Beetle? *Are there*, Beetle?'

Beetle hesitated.

'No,' he said. 'No ghosts. Nothing. Don't be stupid, Kiley.'

'I'm not stupid. You are. And I'm not going nowhere where there's ghosts and spooks and – and . . .'

'There *aren't* any,' said Beetle. 'I was just asking your gran . . .'

'And you said she said—'

'Oh for goodness' sake!'

Beetle flung away, ran up a couple of stairs and turned, stretching one arm to the rail and the other to the wall, pressing them apart till he hung with his feet dangling. Then he dropped down with a plop that made Kiley blink.

'There is no ghost backstage at The Hall. Will you listen? I'm telling you. Watch my lips, Kiley. No – ghost – backstage at The Hall. Nor in the dressing-rooms. Nor in the kitchen. Nor in the passage. Nor on the stairs. Nor . . .'

His voice grew louder and louder. Kiley looked at him, the corners of her mouth turned down and her eyes large.

'Nor anywhere?'

Beetle took a large breath and whipped his hastily crossed fingers behind him.

'Nor anywhere.'

Kiley still looked sceptical. She grabbed her mother's hand and twisted a sausage curl with the other. She rocked backwards and forwards, her tap shoes clicking, her knees, chubby and pink, still tightly clenched. She was still ready to turn and run.

Ben crouched beside her, disentangled the ringlet hand and took it in his.

'But even if there was a ghost – and there *isn't* – there are lots and lots of you together and Miss James will be with you all the time. Your mum's here too. I don't think ghosts like crowds, do you?'

Kiley's knees began to relax and she removed her glare from Beetle to look down at Ben.

'Listen,' said Ben. 'You wouldn't want to spoil the show, would you, Kiley?'

Kiley didn't offer any opinion about that.

'Just think. All those hours you've been practising, you and the others. And what about poor Miss James and all her hard work?'

A little frown of uncertainty passed over the pudgy forehead.

'If you go and do your dance, the others will too, Kiley. Just think how brave they'll think you are.'

'We-e-ell.'

With bad timing, her mother gave her a gentle shake.

'Come on, love,' she said.

Kiley swung round and hid her face against her mother's legs, shaking her head wildly.

It bugged him, but suddenly, Beetle knew the answer.

'Huh,' he said. 'I knew it. Mr Wilson said you were a proper little trouper, but I knew you weren't. Just a cowardy, cowardy custard you are, Kiley Smith. You're not a proper little trouper at all, just a wimp, letting the whole show down just because you're scared of a stupid *ghost*.'

He turned and started to stump up the stairs. Like a flash, Kiley wrenched herself away from her mother and screamed at him.

'Oh no I'm not. I'm not a wimp, so there. I'm a proper little trouper. Not like you, you horrible fish-faced old – old – I'll show you. Just you watch.'

And pulling free of her mother's hand she marched down the passage into the big back room where the other children were still waiting in a state of turmoil. From the passage, Beetle, Ben and her mother heard her voice at top decibels.

'Come on, you lot. Shut up, will you, and listen to me. I'm a proper little trouper, I am, and I'm going to dance in this show and so are you. Catch any ghost trying to stop me.'

There was dead silence, then a shuffling and clipping of tap shoes and then Miss James' voice, high with relief, jollying them along, herding them all towards the dressing-rooms. Kiley's mum gave a kind of 'humph', glared at Beetle and followed them. Ben leant against the wall and ran his hand through his hair.

'Thank God for that,' he said. 'You got us into it, and you got us out, I guess, so let's say no more about it. And I mean that. The word ghost is off the list, taboo, verboten. Understand?'

Beetle nodded.

'Go on. Get on upstairs. I've switched on at the mains. You sit at that desk and come hell or high water you stay there.'

Beetle nodded again, lips pressed tight together.

'And over the intercom, nothing but the show – professional. OK?'

'OK.'

No problem with that. He'd be much too busy for anything else. Back straightened for business, he took the stairs smartly, one at a time at speed, instead of leaping up anyhow. He passed the door on the landing without so much as a glance. Anyone could see he had his mind on essentials. Any ghost of any kind up on the balcony or anywhere else for that matter, would be totally and utterly ignored.

Chapter 13

'House lights go. Stand by Q1.'

'House gone. Standing by.'

The auditorium went dark.

'Go Q1. Stand by Q2.'

'Q1 gone. Standing by.'

The beautiful familiar rhythm of the phrases he thought he'd never hear again seemed to take Beetle over. A warm, serene feeling, with a mixture of excitement and elation bubbling away underneath, welled up inside him. He was at home. Mind on his cross-fades, he hung his sweatshirt over the back of his chair, checked the plot and smiled down at the stage like an old friend. The upward curve of light on the blue curtain made it look as if it was smiling back.

'Go Q2.'

'Q2 gone.'

The piano banged out the fanfare and Greg bustled in, jumping on to his podium exactly at the dawn of his rose-pink light. Not bad timing. Nearly as good as Mr Daniels.

Greg began his patter. He seemed to direct it straight up at Beetle. Had someone told Greg he was up here, nearer to heaven than he'd ever be again? Beetle wasn't sure. He knew Greg couldn't see him, but threw him a grin anyway, all anger and hurt forgotten.

Ben's voice came over the headphones.

'Stand by Q3.'

'Standing by.'

The show slipped into a satisfying and inevitable order and Beetle slipped from cue to cue without a pause. Quiet shadows lurked in the background on the balcony like dark sentinels watching over him, held at bay by the aura of concentration around him.

Reflections from Jamey's silver Indian clubs flew across the distant ceiling and all round the balconies, wheeling and glittering. From far below in the auditorium, Brian cackled loudly at one of the Wilson Brothers' jokes. Beetle thought he probably hadn't understood it, but never mind, it was a first. The tap-dance children, perhaps a little shaky and one or two with eyes red from crying, bobbed up and down in a brave attempt to keep in time. Sequins shimmering, Kiley was clearly in charge, baring her teeth in a grin at the others to inspire them to smile too, and she nudged one or two back into the right place none too gently when they got out of line. Over the headphones, Beetle could just make out Miss James' voice encouraging them from the wings.

Beetle set up the cue for the steel band and sat back to enjoy it. Their act lasted about ten minutes with only one big change of lighting state near the end when the colour wheel started to revolve, turning rainbows into rainbows into rainbows. The band was irresistible. Rita's golden grin and their bouncing rhythms were so infectious they had Beetle bopping about on his seat and tapping his fingers on the desk. But just as they were building up to the climax of their last but one number, he felt a cold draught round the back of his neck. He put up their last cue and glanced round. The balcony was still. In spite of himself, he peered down towards the far end. Empty. He shook himself. There were bound to be draughts up here in this old place. And even if she did come, he wouldn't move. He was certain deep down now that whatever else she was, she wasn't real, so she could neither hurt nor be hurt. If she appeared he would ignore her. If she fell, well, he wouldn't like it, it would be difficult, but he would stay where he was.

He bent his head to put Greg's lighting up for his introduction for Tamar. The cue was a moment or two coming and he sat tensely, his hand on the dimmer, listening for Ben. Nothing must go wrong this time. The cold draught came again, swirling past him, making him shiver, but he kept his head down, concentrating fiercely.

The cue came and went, and he stood by for the next at the beginning of Tamar's act. He must get it right. Slowly and carefully, he slid into the cross-fade and the beautiful, moody lighting Zak had designed for her flowered and held her in its tight circle. She stood quite still, gazing out into the auditorium, her hair a shining black ripple around her shoulders. She started her slow clapping rhythm and Beetle let out a long breath.

All at once, another draught of cold air seemed to envelop him. Without taking his eyes from the stage, he reached behind him for his sweatshirt. Shivering now, he groped about without looking behind him. Suddenly, he froze, cold as stone.

In the dark, another hand took his own and held it.

This was no little girl's hand. This was bigger than his own, thin and hard and rough.

' 'Ullo, *darlin'*. Want to hold hands then, do you?'

Nick Spitz.

He wrenched Beetle's arm up behind him. As Beetle cried out in pain, Pasty White reached out from the shadows and yanked off the head-set. Nick Spitz whipped out his knife and Beetle recoiled.

'Oh don't worry,' said Nick Spitz, with a snigger but keeping his voice low. 'This ain't for you. Not yet. We'll see to you later. We got other plans right now.'

He handed the knife to Pasty White.

'Here,' he said, nodding at the head-set. 'Do it.'

Pasty sawed at the connecting wire of the head-set till it broke. Cut off from Ben, Beetle was alone on the balcony with the two of them. Perhaps if he yelled loud enough . . .

'Oh no,' said Nick Spitz, reading his mind. He took the knife back and held it at Beetle's neck, still holding his arm behind him.

'Now you just sit still. You just sit very, very still.'

'What about—'

'Never mind the show. We'll take care of that, don't you worry.'

He gave another little snigger, but the hand holding the knife was steady. Below them, in another world it seemed, Tamar was going into a new number, but the lighting wasn't due to change for her next two songs.

After that, there should be a cue. Surely, Ben would realize then that something was wrong? He'd know Beetle wouldn't screw up on Tamar a second time.

Pasty White had picked up a large carrier bag just inside the doors and was picking his way down to the front of the balcony. Then he started to edge along the side between the rail and the front row of benches.

'You can't—'

'Oh yes he can, who's gonna stop him?'

'But it's dangerous.'

'Oh yeah? I don't think so, nancy boy, I think you're having us on.'

And ever so slightly, Nick Spitz increased the pressure of the knife against Beetle's neck. Pasty White began to delve into the bag and range the fruit on the bench. Fruit. Rotten fruit. They were for Tamar. They were going to pelt Tamar with rotten fruit from up here. And by the time anyone on stage knew what was happening, they'd be down the stairs and away. Beetle swung round.

'You bastards—'

But the knife met him. He closed his eyes. He had promised Zak. He had promised – and now this. He clenched his fingers in helpless rage, when suddenly he heard it.

Tamar was singing still, but so too was another voice on the stage – that other woman, the woman in purple, singing that other song he had heard yesterday, when the whole place had seemed to be swinging in and out of focus around him. He tried to turn his head to look down at the stage but the knife was still too close.

'Here, what's happening?'

Pasty's hoarse whisper came from below them as he looked back along the balcony at them, puzzled.

'There's someone else singing. Look,' he said.

Nick Spitz nudged Beetle forward with the knife, forcing him down towards the rail. The cold wind was seeping round them steadily now and Beetle looked down towards the end of the balcony.

Please, let *her* be there.

Nothing. No girl in white. Just grey, silent shadows in the gloom. But below, in the auditorium, dark figures drifted in and out of focus – just as on the stage, the voices surged and faded in a cacophony of sounds that sometimes clashed and sometimes rose in harmony, sounds that were strange, chilling.

'What's going on?'

Nick Spitz hissed in Beetle's ear.

'Dunno,' said Beetle, with a ring of truth. 'I dunno.'

Pasty White looked uncertain as he stood with a

large rotten pear in his hand. Two figures stood on the stage. Tamar and the woman in the purple dress seemed to slide in and out of each other in the spotlight. Each time he raised his hand to aim at Tamar, she seemed to disappear and the woman stood there, pointing at the audience, swaying her hips, pouting.

'Who's she, for Chrissake?'

But, just as she had done the day before, suddenly the woman in purple vanished and the auditorium was still and empty. Pasty raised an arm.

'No!'

Beetle's voice rang out but Nick Spitz's hand, reeking of stale tobacco, clamped over his mouth, making him retch.

'Shut it!'

Suddenly, Beetle saw her. She was there, the little girl was there, reaching down to where the woman had been. With his whole body Beetle gestured down towards the side of the balcony, his eyes nearly popping from his head in an effort to make Nick Spitz see her too.

'What?' said Pasty White, his attention taken from the stage. 'What's he on about?' he said to Nick Spitz.

'That kid down there,' said Nick Spitz. 'What about her?'

He took his hand from Beetle's mouth but kept the knife close, very close. The little girl was leaning forward, her arms through the rails.

'She'll fall,' said Beetle, with a gasp. 'Get her. Get her back.'

'Tough,' said Nick Spitz. 'Go on, Pasty. Get on with it. The Turkish bird's nearly finished down there.'

Tamar was just going into her last song. The lights should have changed.

'Look!' said Beetle, trying to keep his voice low. 'The kid shouldn't be up here. She's going to fall, look. Pasty – you can't let her fall. She'll be killed. Get her back.'

The little girl leant out further and further. For a moment undecided, Pasty dropped the pear and started to lumber on down the balcony towards her. Nick tightened his hold on Beetle but watched Pasty go.

'Hey, kid, don't do that. Oi, come here.'

With eyes like great gaunt hollows, the little girl looked round as Pasty drew nearer. She seemed to press herself against the balcony rail. He stumbled over a bench, recovered himself, then fell towards her, arms outstretched to catch her. The rail seemed to dissolve. With a cry, the child passed through it and dropped down and down, tumbling over and over through the beams of light. Her cry ripped out into the vast empty space, echoing and receding, but the sound of her hitting the ground never came. The noise of Pasty going through the floor of the balcony must have drowned it.

The balcony doors burst open.

'What the hell's going on up here?'

Zak stood in the doorway.

In a flash, Nick Spitz whipped the knife behind him, but not before Zak had seen it.

'Give it here.'

'Come and get it.'

Zak hurled himself down the steps but Nick pulled Beetle in front of him and thrust the knife towards his throat.

'Oh no. Any nearer and I'll cut him.'

Zak stopped dead. Beetle felt the faint tremble of the knife against his flesh and smelled the sweat of fear as Nick Spitz slowly began to edge his way past Zak. Feeling each step behind him with his feet and keeping his eyes on Zak, Nick half lifted, half dragged Beetle up the steps towards the doors. Zak turned with them, and started to follow, but slowly, slowly. Nearer and nearer the doors they edged, Nick and Beetle, locked together, the knife glittering as they passed in and out of shadows. Off balance, both arms trapped by one of Nick's, the knife at his throat, Beetle could do nothing but stumble upwards with him.

The doors burst open and Ben stood silhouetted against the light.

'What the—?'

'He's got a knife!'

Zak sprang forward as Nick swung round, the knife flying upwards, grazing Beetle's cheek.

Ben grabbed his elbows from behind and Zak lunged forward and twisted his wrist till the knife fell to the floor. Beetle dropped to his knees and reached for it as it rolled away under a bench.

'Get on the intercom and get Rita and the guys up here. And tell someone to call the police.'

Ben and Zak were struggling to keep Nick Spitz from bolting down the stairs.

'They cut the wires.'

'Damn them!'

'I'll go!'

Greg appeared in the doorway, took one look at what was happening, and leapt away downstairs again. Beetle lay panting under the bench, wiping his forehead with a dusty hand, hanging on to the knife but shaking all over.

Rita, Yip and Buster arrived and manhandled

Nick away down the stairs to wait for the police. Already Beetle could hear the approach of distant sirens outside. He got to his knees, crawled out from under the bench and stood up.

Zak put an arm round his shoulder.

'You OK?'

Beetle nodded. He looked at Ben.

'I couldn't help it. They came up behind me. And then they cut the wire. I couldn't . . .'

'Of course not. It's OK, Beetle. You did fine.'

'They?' said Zak. 'Both up here, were they? Then where's the other one?'

Beetle gave a little laugh and jerked his thumb away down the balcony.

'I forgot. He's down there.'

Ben and Zak stared along the balcony but could see nothing. Suddenly they heard a groan.

Gingerly, Zak picked his way across the benches. He stood looking down for a moment, then called back:

'Hey, Ben. If you thought you'd got a hole in your balcony before, you should see this one. He's down here on the floor below, without a lift. Hello, young Pasty. Been practising your parachuting then, have you?'

There was only a faint moan in reply.

Chapter 14

For the second time in twenty-four hours, the ambulance had snaked through the quiet streets to The Hall and taken away another patient for Greg's mum at the local hospital, this one accompanied by a policeman. Pasty White had a broken leg, a bang on the head and probably broken ribs too. Nick Spitz was on his way elsewhere, in quite a different vehicle. Zak had fixed the intercom, the worst of the mess on the balcony had been cleared up and the hole covered temporarily with back-cloth scrim. The audience wouldn't be allowed on to the lower balcony but the show could go on. Rita and the band had stayed to help and Brian had had a great time with vacuum cleaners, dustpans, hammers and nails while Yip and Buster nudged him and kidded him into paroxysms of giggles, egged on by Rita. Now they were gone, and Brian was dispensing tea with enthusiasm unabated. The people remaining in the kitchen dodged the splashes as he reached across them with fistfuls of mugs. For once, Old Mitch, exhausted, sat and let him get on with it.

Beetle, grime on his face, on his hands, and just about everywhere else, sat between Greg and Zak.

'I thought you were coming tomorrow – and only maybe.'

'The band had a night off and Ben sounded pretty urgent, so I thought I'd get here if I could. I hitched a lift from Coventry right down to the roundabout. Bit of luck.'

'I'll say,' said Ben. 'I knew something was wrong up there, but not those two – I thought it was just you screwing up again, Beetle – sorry!'

Beetle just gave a grin and rubbed the back of his neck. Dust trickled down his back.

'It wasn't too bad till then, was it?' he said.

'It was brilliant,' said Ben.

Greg gave Beetle a gentle elbow in the ribs and Tamar, sitting next to her mother opposite Zak, smiled and said:

'You know, Beetle, I didn't even notice there was anything strange happening at all until the lights stayed on when I had finished – and then I saw Ben wasn't in the corner.'

'Shows the kind of singer you are,' said Zak.

'Insensitive?' said Tamar.

'No,' said Zak fiercely, looking straight at her. 'Just so concentrated the world could fall round your ears and you'd carry on, like – like . . .'

He dropped his head and looked away quickly. Tamar gave a puzzled little frown.

'Oh. Is that good?'

'It's good,' said Zak. 'Believe me, it's good.'

'You mean, like a proper little trouper?' said Beetle. Greg groaned.

'Hey, man, let's leave Kiley out of it, huh?' he said. 'Well, at least we don't have to tail you everywhere now, Tamar. No way those two are going to give you grief for a while.'

'You have been very kind,' said Tamar, and her mother nodded.

'Pasty wasn't so bad,' said Beetle.

'Huh? You're joking?' said Greg. 'He was just as—'

'No,' said Beetle. 'He didn't go for me with the knife.'

He took a deep breath. If ever the business of the ghost was going to be cleared up, it was now, even if they did think he was a nutter.

'And – and he was trying to save the – the little girl when he went through the floor.'

'The what? Oh, not that again, Beetle,' said Ben.

'She was there,' said Beetle, firmly. 'Just as he was going to start chucking all that rotten stuff at Tamar and I couldn't move because of the knife, she was there. Just before that, there was something funny going on with the lights and the sound on stage, like there was last night – only I couldn't say with Mr Daniels going to hospital and all. But all that happened again, and then the kid was there, reaching over the railing just like the other times. But tonight, when Pasty tried to get to her to stop her, she fell. I heard her scream. Oh she was there all right, trust me. She saved my life.'

'Well, where is she now then?' said Ben. 'I didn't see any little heap in the auditorium.'

'No,' said Old Mitch. He sighed. 'They say she never reaches the ground. She'll be, well, I couldn't say where she is now, but I reckon she was there, Beetle – and on the other times too. But only you could see her and, thank God, tonight, somehow Pasty White must have seen her too.'

'Not ghosts again,' said Ben.

'Well, you can believe what you like,' said Old Mitch. 'I didn't say anything before because of the kids. But there are stories.'

'Like what?' said Beetle.

'I've never seen her, but they say that a long time

ago a little girl was up there on the balcony watching her mother on stage, singing some old music hall song I suppose. *My Old Man Said Follow the Van* or something. It was during a performance and there was a big audience. It was the days when you could take your beer and whelks in with you. The kid got out of the dressing-room somehow and went up the back stairs. When she saw her mum, she leant way out through the railings and fell. Ever since then, they say if you see her, it's a kind of warning. Only one person ever sees her – the person she is trying to warn.'

'Me,' said Beetle. 'And those other times too. Not just here you know – other places. Even outside. She must have been trying to warn me about Nick Spitz and Pasty. Poor little . . .'

'Yes,' said Tamar, sadly. 'Poor little girl. Having to come back and live through it all again whenever someone's in danger.'

'Or maybe it wasn't me, but you. It was always during your act I saw her,' said Beetle, 'and once, when you were on your own in the auditorium, or just before I was going to meet you. Well, whoever – she knew . . . she knew . . . somehow, she knew about those two and what they meant to do.'

There was silence for a moment, then Brian said:

'New . . . new . . . new . . . New tea?'

A little smile faltered round the room and Old Mitch shook himself and got up.

'No, Brian. That's enough. We've got the show tomorrow. You've done wonders tonight, old lad, but it's time to go home now.'

There was a general stretching and pushing back of chairs.

'About tomorrow,' said Ben. 'Zak'll be here, Beetle, but if you really want to, I guess I could bend the rules just one more time . . .'

'Yeah,' said Beetle with a grin. 'I think you can say I really want to.'

And he and Zak slapped hands West Indian style.

'Washing up can wait till tomorrow,' said Old Mitch, shooing everyone towards the door.

'I'll lock up, Mitch,' said Ben. 'You go on.'

They thronged up the passage and out through the doors, where a small crowd was gathered, discussing the significance of ambulances and police cars at The Hall. Old Mitch spotted Brian's carer pushing his way towards them and delivered him up with a pat on the back and a 'nighty-night, old lad'. Brian trotted off arm in arm with his carer with words like 'teeee' and 'nails, bang, bang' floating back on the night air. Old Mitch wagged his head with a tired smile.

Kiley's gran was there, deep in conference with her Bingo cronies. She hurried over and lifted Beetle's chin with her hand.

'You OK, love?' she said. Beetle nodded.

'They said it was you he hurt, that – that . . .'

'Nah. Close. But I'm OK.'

'Better be,' said Kiley's gran with a sniff. Zak put both his hands on Beetle's shoulders.

Just then Greg's nan arrived. She was tightly clasped in a navy-blue polka-dotted dress with a swirly skirt and gold buttons, and a little flat hat perched at a rakish angle over one eye. She elbowed her way through the crowd, grabbed hold of him and said:

'I heard someone talking up the street. What's all this about ambulances and knives, child?'

'All over now,' said Greg. 'You should have seen Beetle. Big fight. Cool, man.'

Greg's nan cuffed his ear, fondly.

'Cool? That's not cool, that's terrible. You all right, child?' she said, turning to Beetle. 'My, you look awful. Skinny bit of a thing. You need a good meal by the look of you.'

'That's what she always says,' said Greg, with a grin. 'But hey, can he come home and eat with us? His old lady won't mind, will she?'

Beetle shook his head.

'Mind? She probably won't even notice, but I'd better go home and tell her, just in case.'

'I'll push a note through your door to let her know,' said Kiley's gran. 'You go on with Greg and have a bit of a fuss made of you, love. Go on. I'll take care of it.'

'What about all the stairs up to mine?'

Old Mitch cleared his throat.

'If you'll allow me, I'll go with you, ma'am. It'll be a pleasure.'

'Uh oh,' said Greg, and Kiley's gran flapped at him with her handbag, but she went a bit pink just the same.

'He can tell you all about the *ghost*,' said Beetle. 'You know, the one that doesn't exist?'

Kiley's gran had the grace to go a little pinker.

'All right, all right,' she said as she set off with Old Mitch, 'but not a word to Kiley, do you hear?'

'No problem,' said Beetle, calling after them. 'Not speaking to Kiley is *no* problem.'

Greg laughed.

'Too right, man,' he said.

Kiley's gran shook her head and tutted as she turned the corner but Beetle could tell she was laughing. Zak was still standing behind Beetle with his hands on his shoulders.

'Can Zak come too?' said Beetle to Greg's nan.

' 'S OK,' said Zak. 'Go ahead. I'll see you tomorrow. I'm going to take Tamar and her mother home.'

'But we don't need—' said Tamar.

'I know you don't need . . .' said Zak. 'I'm just going to walk you home because – because . . .'

'Let him come,' said her mother. Tamar looked surprised. Her mother said something to her in Kurdish and she dropped her head shyly, her veil slipping forward and covering her face. With a wink, Zak walked off between them. Beetle and Greg nudged each other.

'Think it's catching?' said Beetle. 'What about you and Kiley, then?'

Greg was about to jump him, when his nan interrupted.

'Oh yes, lots of energy is it?' she said, putting one hand on her hip and the other on his collar. 'And where's your costume Gregory Emmanuel? I thought I told you—'

'Gregory *Emmanuel*?' said Beetle, in disbelief.

'Shut it, man, just shut it,' said Greg, giving him a punch. 'Don't you ever, ever tell anyone . . .'

'That's enough,' said his nan. 'You stop that right

now. It's a fine name and you just be proud of it, you hear? And where's your costume? I want to give it a clean up and a press for the show.'

Beetle grinned as Greg turned back to The Hall, but Ben was already putting the key in his pocket. Everything was locked up.

'It's OK, Nan,' said Greg. 'Costume's fine. Let's eat.'

And on his way to the pub, Ben watched them down the road with a smile as they danced on and off the pavements, Greg's nan behind them on her high heels, swinging her hips till her skirt seemed to have a life of its own.

'Chicken and rice,' she was saying, 'and cinnamon apple pie for afters.'

Beetle sat beside Zak up on the balcony for the whole of the show. Tomorrow he was going to see Mr Daniels in hospital, but now he watched as, effortlessly, Zak slid the cues one to the other. The show was the best ever. It had to be said that the Wilson Brothers had done about as well as usual, but Kiley and her little mates had bounced through the dancing-class number, sparkling away, bunches bobbing, and the audience had murmured words like 'a-a-a-ah' and 'ever so cute'. Rita and the band had brought the house down. And now it was Tamar's turn. Zak brought up the dimmers on Greg in all his finery. He beamed up at them and at the end of his announcement, clasped his hands together above his head and pumped them up and down. Zak slipped out of his seat and pushed Beetle into his place.

'Go on,' he said. 'Your turn. Time you got it right, for once.'

'For once?' said Beetle. 'Huh.'

He pushed back his sleeves, bent his head over the cue-sheets, looked down at the stage and slowly and smoothly pushed up one dimmer and pulled down the other till the lights cross-faded like butter in the sun.

'Cool,' said Zak. 'See? Told you.'

'Uh-huh,' said Beetle, with a sideways nod of his head. 'No sweat, man. No sweat at all.'

Then suddenly, just for a moment, he wondered.

He glanced across down the dark, empty balcony, where for all he knew, a bit of his knee still stuck to the floorboards. Nothing moved. The shadows were still. Only tiny dust motes drifted dreamily on the beam from the lamp Zak had changed all that time ago. Far below them, in her circle of golden light, Tamar started to sing.